To Jane

MISCEL

Thank you for everything!

Enjoy Miscellany?

Andrew Lamont

AL

Andrew Lamont

AUTHOR'S NOTE

This book has been a long time in the making. Writing these stories, compiling them into this book has changed my life. There are triggers within the pages of this book, including miscarriage, the loss of a spouse, the loss of friends, guilt.

Writing these stories has helped me enormously with so many things. I hope you enjoy reading them as much as I enjoyed writing them. Thank you so much for coming on this journey with me.

Contents

Lady Tabitha's Revenge

Dedicated to Ben Alderson, a great friend, role model, and person.

Beauty holds darkness in its hand, shelters it, pushes out the light. This is especially true when it comes to the grand castles in the hills of rural Scotland.

Behind the prettily aged bricks, the gorgeous staircases, the beautiful portraits of owners long since dead, the amazing weight of the history of the estate, lies an evil the world will only recognise when it is too late.

I beg you, dear reader, believe me when I tell you the evil I am going to tell you about truly exists. It lurks in shadowed corners, loiters in pitch black alleyways, lingers in the gloom. It watches you, stalks you, waiting for the perfect moment.

I have desperately longed to tell my story, but have always lacked the courage. Now, as I lie on my deathbed, I have reached my final chance. Without telling my story, I cannot go to my grave and rest. Even then, I expect my soul will never find peace.

I implore you, dear reader, forgive me ...

***

At the age of seventeen, I entered the world of employment for the first time. Living in a small town in rural Scotland, positions were relatively easy to come by. I knew the people who managed the castle and they gave me it before I even asked about work.

Naive excitement bubbled through me as I walked to the castle on the first day. Nothing could have prepared me for what was going to happen. Who could have predicted? Nobody. Who could have believed it? Nobody. Who would have believed me? Nobody. So I remained silent.

Being seventeen and infinitely innocent, I thought people were joking when they spoke of the hauntings at McAvoy Castle. No-one in their right mind would have believed them. And I certainly didn't. If only trust came easily to me, I would never have gone to work there. Only two people – the Laurences – tried to warn me about the dangers of going to work at McAvoy's Castle.

They were never people to talk much sense though. They had only gone to the castle once too and that was before I was born. For the rest of their lives, they stayed away.

Professing to me that I mustn't ever work there, they simply looked, and sounded, deranged, muttering something about my grandfather who died a few months before I turned five. I never thought much of that talk again until it was too late.

Since it was my first day in the job, I was assigned to clean the library.

Positively giddy with joy at the prospect of working, I charged like an overjoyed child into the room.

It all began in that library. That condemned, yet beautiful room. Crimson carpets of crimson, mahogany shelves, books in perfect condition, even after decades. Everything in there had stayed in a state of perfection, most likely due to a lack of use. Oh, and thanks to how well the contents were looked after.

Dusting the magnificent bookshelves, perusing the titles of the great tomes as I did so, I heard a creak. Turning around, I saw nothing out of the ordinary. Working in an aged castle, one expects to hear strange noises like that, so my mind wandered happily back to the books.

However, when I heard it again mere moments later, I was convinced it was some sort of initiation. The majority of employees there were fully-grown adults, but possessed the immaturity of youth. We were all my friends though and they knew me well enough to know I seldom got scared. I had no doubt in my mind that they wanted to see how long it would take for fear to trickle into my blood and pulse relentlessly through me.

At the age of seventeen, I was fearless though. It was a gift that grew to be a burden. Determined not to let my colleagues have a laugh at my expense, I returned to my dusting. "You can stop!" I shouted. "You are not scaring me." I smiled. After all, I was earning my own money at long last. It was a beautiful day outside, I was amongst friends. I had so much to smile about.

Hearing laughter from outside, I chucked the duster onto the sofa and made my way over to the window, pushing the aged sash up with difficulty, and, rather like I dog, I poked my head out. Odd, I thought to myself. All of my colleagues were outside.

That was when the creaking sounded again. This time it sounded like floorboards. I felt breathing on the back of my neck, then an icy waft of air. I swerved round, sensing something. I was alone ...

Of course you're alone, I remember thinking. Just then, a black feather floated down from the ceiling and landed next to my feet. Picking it up, I thought nothing of it. After all, it was just a feather. It meant nothing. Little did I know that I had just received my first warning.

An almighty crash sounded so that I jumped. My heart nearly jumped out of my chest at the sheer volume. A flash of white caught my eye, followed by a shadow disappearing into the next room.

I decided to play along and followed it into the bedroom. Whoever is playing these tricks has made a mistake, I thought. Having grown up with this castle as the only family-day-out location within a fifty-mile radius, I knew every corner: whoever was trying to frighten me had gone into the nursery and the only way out was through the door I had just walked through.

Baby blue wallpaper, pear-green carpets, demonic dolls lining the walls. I'd never liked those horrid things with their glassy little eyes … I had always felt like they were watching me. Even as a child. Little china boys and girls, expensively made, no doubt, especially back then. I, for one, would not spend a penny on them though. They *still* give me nightmares. Thank goodness the fashion for toys had changed. Although, in my town fashion was still an embarrassment.

Shivers ran down my spine then, however —not through fear, but through a sudden drop in temperature. As I walked through the door, I might as well have thrown myself into the loch: it would have been warmer.

At that moment, I thought nothing of it. I mean, the nursery had never been particularly warm.

Looking around, confusion mingled with irritation: not a soul occupied the room apart from mine.

Obstinacy grabbed me. "Nah," I said to myself. "There is no such thing as ghosts. It is an old building. My imagination is playing tricks on me."

Despite my stubbornness, I could not deny the sudden realisation that my arm hair was standing on end. *It must be the cold*, I thought dismissively. Why was it so cold?

"Don't be daft, Kathleen," I snapped at myself. "You are in Scotland. Be it the middle of winter, or the middle of summer, it will be freezing."

As I finished voicing common sense, there was another excruciatingly loud crash from the library, so loud it could have been an explosion.

Turning to leave, I found the source of that almighty crash was the nursery door slamming.

I can't have shut the window properly.

"For goodness sake," I muttered, my irritation beginning to grow. Venomous fear slithered into my heart though as I turned the handle: the door was locked.

Creak. Creak.

I twisted my neck round, hoping that, despite all my years spent coming to this castle, I had overlooked a second exit. Of course, I hadn't.

I wish I had not turned around: if I hadn't, I would never have had the overwhelming sensation that those cursed dolls were watching me. I know now that it was no sensation. I know now that ever since I was employed at that repugnant place, I had been chosen for the demon's revenge on the world.

The truth is too much to bear. Reality often is. Nevertheless, I will tell it. I have hidden for too long. It will be known. Just not yet.

I tried the doorknob several times, each time more vigorously than the last.

What is happening?

The curtains swished shut. The cold deepened, turning my blood to icy water. I could see my breath pouring out of me.

A scream. Sadistic laughter. And then the door opened.

I ran back into the library. The window was open, blowing cold air through the room. I walked over and closed it. I chastised myself, endeavouring to regain control of my pounding heart.

I knew I was being childish for allowing myself to be frightened, to be tricked somehow. Besides, curtains could not close themselves.

Feeling heat on the back of my head, I swerved round and they were open. I had imagined the whole thing. At least that is what I told myself.

But that was my second warning.

I continued dusting the bookshelves, quicker than before.

Even at the top of the castle, I heard the staff door banging shut. How could I not have? Everyone in Scotland would have heard that. Even those lying in their graves.

Creak. I scanned the room. *Nothing there, of course*, I thought to myself.

But I was wrong. Swinging sullenly from side to side was the portrait of Lord Earl McAvoy. His eyes fixed on me.

I would *not* be tricked. I would *not* be fearful. Fear is just an illusion. There would be a logical explanation. No matter what was happening, there would be a logical explanation. *Surely.* There always is.

"Stop it now!" I bellowed down the stairs.

Obviously, anger played no part in it: this castle was colossal, bigger than any I had seen or heard about from others. "Could you come up here please?"

Two minutes passed and the portrait still swung on its hook. Not that I was scared by this point, but I could not shake the feeling that Lord McAvoy was watching me with cruel eyes. His eyes were not just cruel though, they were cold, emotionless, dead. Yet, watching. I had always found the blank expression that rested eternally upon his face to be unsettling. Most people in our small town did. Nobody could explain why his face was so unnerving. His features just had a knack of making everyone feel uncomfortable.

Eventually, after what felt like several years, my colleagues waltzed into the library, grinning. "What's the matter, Kathleen?" Bradley Elliot enquired.

Bradley Elliot was a year older than me. His chocolate-brown hair matched his bark brown eyes. He was of medium build. Bradley was incredibly bright, but leant more towards emotion than logic. Although he towered over me, I knew he looked up to me: he often came to me for advice. Even though he was older than me, he was no more than a child.

"Nothing," I answered instantly, not wanting to tell them all what I had just witnessed. Maybe if I had, they would still be alive? Maybe. My life is a collection of maybes. I was being ridiculous. I knew I was. I did not need to be told, however, I wanted reassurance.

"Why did you call us up then?" Malcolm Findlay snapped. "We have work to do." I could not stand that creature. He was petulant, impetuous, ostentatious with his family's money and he had an over-inflated self-worth.

Malcolm's personality was not down to him though. A product of his upbringing, he believed he was entitled to everything he desired.

I tried so hard not to judge him harshly. He did not choose his life any more than he chose to die the way he did. But words cannot explain how repellent he was. I, by no means, am glad for what happened to him though. Nobody deserves that. But, we are not at that point of the story yet. Bear with me, reader.

"Was it the painting?" Anne Cooke questioned. "Was it swaying like a ship in a storm again? Cascading from side to side? It tends to do that. Don't think anything of it."

Anne was one who always saw the best in situations. She had a talent for making things sound dramatic and yet still unimportant. Although she tended to look for the bright side of everything, it was most irritating. She was a lovely lady though in many ways and I miss her deeply. Her love for the castle was unmatched. Nobody ever understood why she adored it so much. She was fifty-six and had been working there since she was fifteen. I was the only one she told about why she refused to stop working in that forsaken place. However, that is a part of the story we will get to nearer the end.

"It was the portrait obviously," Harold Manson said, coughing. He smoked more than anyone I knew and had done for longer than I had been alive. Harold was a nice enough person, but quite abrupt. He was never unpleasant; it was just his manner and everybody knew he meant no offense. Oh, no, Harold would never hurt anybody. I hope he is resting in peace. But I doubt it.

"It wasn't just that," I cut in. "I felt breathing down the back of my neck—"

"You're imagining things," Douglas Mitchell told me. Nobody knew Douglas very well at all. He kept himself to himself. All I knew of him was that he had never married; he must have been a lonely man. Douglas rarely spoke, so everybody looked at him in surprise. Before that day, I do not know if I had ever heard his voice.

He didn't scare me exactly. That's not the correct word. I don't know quite how to explain what I mean other than saying I would have hated to be alone with him.

My judgement of Douglas has been a source of self-loathing since he died. No. He didn't *die*. He was murdered. Douglas never harmed anyone and he never would have.

He was shy, not dangerous. I wish I had made more of an effort to get to know him. All he needed was a friend. I could have been that friend. Instead, I allowed my judgement to set myself apart from him. I more or less ostracised him because he was different. That is something I will never forgive myself for.

"—and I found this black feather at my feet." I held it up. Perhaps to prove I was not just imagining things. Despite everything that had happened – the copious number of what I now know were warning signs – I was not in the slightest bit perturbed. After all, ghosts did not exist.

Not believing in ghosts, I thought nothing of it then. Although, nobody could have expected the excitement that feather created. Anne grabbed it out of my hand and left the room, Douglas sighed and muttered something about idiocy, Bradley looked utterly discombobulated and Harold's eyes widened before he bolted out of the room. That cannot have been good for his lungs.

"What is going on?" Bradley asked.

"Nothing," Malcolm said, suddenly enraged. "It means nothing. It is superstitious nonsense."

"It's a feather," I said impudently. "Of course, it means nothing! What could it mean?"

Creak. I glanced irately up at the portrait of Lord McAvoy. Odd, I thought. It was not moving.

"What's creaking?" I asked anybody who would answer. For some unfathomable reason, when I was alone, I was unshaken. However, now that I had people around me, I could not shake the feeling that I was being watched by some malevolent presence.

There was that sensation again! My hairs stood up on end. I tried to push them down, but I couldn't: they were sharp as thorns.

"What's *that*?" Bradley stuttered, his voice riddled with anxiety. He lifted his finger and pointed towards the nursery.

I rolled my eyes. "How stupid do you think I am?" I snapped, irritation dominating my voice. I mean, let's be sensible. That trick may have worked if I had been five years old. "I'm not turning around."

"Impossible." It was Bradley who spoke again. The minutiae of his face added up to one thing: incredulity.

Parenthetically, I want to make it clear that I only turned around because of the speed at which Bradley's face drained of colour. Paler than death, he stared.

I succumbed to my curiosity. Then my legs collapse beneath me.

In front of us stood a heavily pregnant woman in an intricate and gorgeous wedding dress. But ... something was wrong.

Red coated her dress from the stomach down. Having grown up in that beautiful building, I recognised her immediately as Lady Tabitha from her great beauty. I've always had a tremendous attraction to danger.

"Lady Tabitha," I murmured. "Wait. *What*?"

Lady Tabitha, the wife of Lord McAvoy, had a very interesting story: born into poverty, married into luxury. The couple had been in love for over a decade before Lord McAvoy's parents had died; they immediately married. If my memory serves, they married the following day. Quite a fairy tale.

Their happiness doubled when Lady Tabitha announced her pregnancy the following month. Celebrations spread through our small town. Lady Tabitha ordered luxurious baby clothes, toys, bedding. The very best, from the most-skilled, in Scotland. Joy ruled. But, as always, the joy was temporary: she lost the baby.

All the glee vanished and our small town was immersed in mourning. Sixty years had passed, but still the story was spoken of in hushed tones.

Full details of Lady Tabitha's miscarriage never came out. Although nobody knew just how awful it was, everybody knew that it was horrific. One day later, Lord McAvoy threw himself from the roof. The same day, Lady Tabitha drowned in the loch.

But there she was. Right in front of me. A ghost. Right there. No. I was over-emotional and imagining things. Everything went fuzzy at the edges as my vision abandoned me and I was submerged in darkness.

***

Surrounded by my colleagues, I awoke in the living room, humiliatingly sprawled across the chaise longue.

"What happened?" I asked, even though I knew the answer: I had *seen* a ghost. Don't be absurd, I thought to myself. Ghosts don't exist. Do they? No. *Surely.* Ghosts are what parents use to frighten their children into going to bed at the right time. I had allowed myself to become emotionally unbalanced. Ridiculous. I was seventeen after all, too old to let myself be frightened by trivial, childish nonsense.

"You fainted. Are you alright? Did you hurt yourself? Do you need a glass of water?" Bradley spoke hurriedly.

Everybody who knew him knew of his love for me. I have always felt an overpowering yet deserved guilt at the fact that I never told him that I felt the same.

"Don't be such a child." It was Douglas who spoke then. "She passed out, it's not like she died." His intonations didn't match his words; it betrayed some kind of concern, however mild that may be. I now know Douglas cared about people like no-one I'd ever come across, but he never showed it. He worried, nonetheless. I still didn't want to be alone with him. He swept out of the room.

"Bradley," I began, hesitantly. I needed to tell him what happened in the nursery. After all, he had seen Lady Tabitha. I was convinced that he would believe me. How could I have told him what had happened without sounding insane though?

Am I insane? The question remained in my mind until the last night I spent in that town.

Bradley asked, "Did you see it too?" His face screamed reluctant belief. "I saw the ghost of Lady Tabitha again. I had convinced myself I had been imagining things."

"I think we were both imagining things, Bradley."

He looked around, presumably to make sure nobody could hear what he was about to say. "I wasn't imagining it. You saw it too!"

I could easily have just been dehydrated. Dehydration was highly plausible. I hadn't had anything to drink since the night before. Glancing at the clock, I was relieved: midday.

"No," I replied. "I was needing a glass of water."

Indignantly, Bradley rolled his eyes. "No. You weren't. You saw it. I saw the look on your face as it appeared."

I sighed and laid back down without saying another word. This could *not* be happening. Surely! The entire affair was a figment of my imagination. I just *knew* it. It had to be. Ghosts were *not* real. But I *had* seen one.

No, I chastised myself. *You didn't. You are acting like a gullible child. You know ghosts don't exist.*

Never in my life had I been so convinced of anything and yet *so* wrong. Irony's cold grip still tightens upon me daily. Especially as I recall how sure I was.

"You were terrified. You were sweating. You couldn't control your breathing. You saw something when you were alone in that library and I want you to tell me what."

I spoke so much, yet said so little.

Fighting back a laugh at how authoritative he suddenly sounded, I sat up. "Okay," I whispered. "But you have to promise not to laugh."

Offense clouded his face. "Why would I laugh? You know I love you and will believe anything you tell me. I promise."

I was not ready to tell him I loved him as well. I never was ready until it was too late. It's not as if I was unaware. I just was not accustomed to feeling that strongly for another person. *What a pathetic excuse. Leaving him in the dark was cruel. All because I didn't feel ready? Selfish.* I loved him more than words could say. Another place, another time, another life. Maybe then we could have been together ... or maybe if I had been less selfish.

I had been telling myself that for the two years I had known of his love. Although, the truth is, we could have been happy if I had been brave enough to tell him what I knew I felt. *Why didn't I?* There had been so many possibilities, several every time I saw him. Why had I not been more courageous? Maybe if I had been, things would have gone differently for me. Maybe, if I had told him I would not be here alone, dying without anyone by my side. Maybe he'd still be alive.

"Not here," I replied. "I'll tell you tonight at Ratchet's Inn."

***

We arranged to meet at seven o'clock that night. Anne had sent me home early due to my fainting episode and, during that afternoon off, I came up with a plan - a plan which would *prove* my point: ghosts do not exist. Never have and never will. To my seventeen-year-old mind, the plan had no flaws. I spent hours that afternoon thinking it through. Everything would be back to normal the next day.

I'd forgotten – or refused to take into consideration – that I could be, and was, wrong.

The stench of smoke and alcohol in Ratchet's Inn was unavoidable. It was always the first thing people noticed, so strong was the odour.

The floors were cobbled, the walls were wooden with several paintings of the seaside and fields scattered across them.

Broken conversations surrounded me. I attempted to choose one to eavesdrop on for entertainment, however they were dull: most of them prattled on about how Mr MacDonald had stolen fifty pounds from his work. As I said, dull. I had known about his illicit activities for months and had quite lost interest.

The clock struck a quarter past. I would have stayed waiting until closing time as Bradley was seldom late. Besides, he was well worth the wait.

Out of the corner of my eye, George McIver could be seen making his way over to me. He was always warm and kind to me, but he hated everybody else. He was a poor soul: his wife had died six years before from cancer and he was going the same way. Everybody knew it apart from him. Well, he knew, but hadn't accepted the truth we all must bear: this life is going to end. He clung to his opinion that Doctor Anderson didn't know what he was speaking about. A retired soldier, George never gave up, always refused to let himself be defeated.

Doctor Anderson had diagnosed him with the vile disease a few weeks before. George was unlucky enough to have a virulent form of the illness. He would be dead within the year.

George, however, was not one to be beaten and he carried on his life as normal, not allowing anybody to treat him. "I don't need it," he would say. He greatly missed his wife, Isobel, and spoke of her often. But he always said, "Not to worry, I'll see her in a few years. I am not dying yet."

"Good evening, George," I said happily. "It's a right fine evening, isn't it?"

As he stumbled closer to me, the smell of alcohol intensified. "Aye," he replied blurredly, "it is that." Looking at him, it was obvious his health had deteriorated even since the weekend. There was no escaping it: George McIver was dying.

"Are you keeping well?" I asked, instantly regretting the question.

"I am," he answered. "What is a bonny lass like you doing here by herself?"

George was genuinely unhappy with the situation. He was not like other men who came over to gloat: he had looked after me as a child when my parents worked and he hated seeing me alone. "I am waiting for Bradley Elliot, George," I told him, smiling as I said his name.

His face lit up like the sky at midnight on New Year's Day. He stood back up and nearly toppled over as he leaned over to give me a hug. "I am happy for you," he whispered into my ear, "but take care of yourself."

I was about to tell him that we were just friends when the clock struck the half hour and Bradley charged into the inn like a terrified cat. "There he is now."

George turned around and waved his stick in the air. "Oi! You!" he bellowed. "You take care of Kathleen, or I'll have your heart for haggis."

He turned back to me, "I'll leave you two alone now."

"Thank you, George," I replied, standing up to hug him goodbye.

I had to fight back the urge to guffaw as he glared furiously at Bradley when wobbling back to his table. Bradley, who knew George well, smiled. He walked over to the table with glee.

When he sat down, I was immersed in silence. Nothing mattered apart from our conversation. Bradley ordered his drink and, as I told him about what had happened, he stared at me with widened eyes. I carried on in the hope that he believed me: if he hadn't, he would have interrupted me. "And that's when I called you all up," I concluded.

"Wow." I nodded, glad he believed me, was there with me and hoping he would agree to my plan. I was optimistic, but unsure. "There's one thing I still do not understand," he said.

"Yes?"

"Why did you not tell me when we were up at the castle?"

Trying to think of an answer other than. "Because I want to be alone with you," was not easy.

"Has Anne left yet?" I asked, ignoring his question.

He nodded, but looked at me questioningly, his mouth twitching. It always did that.

I miss him so much. Why didn't I tell him? Here was another opportunity but, of course, I did not have the courage. Why am I so weak? Why do I always let myself down? Why do I always let others down? I have spent many years wishing I could revisit that day and tell him. If only I could.

"Why are you asking?" he enquired, his anxiety increasing, his confusion deepening. As I have said, Bradley was *intimidatingly* bright: he must have known I was planning to go back up there.

Before answering, I decided not to ask him to help, but I wouldn't stop him either. "*If* there's a ghost, it'll show itself more forcefully at night."

I wasn't sure how I knew this to be true.

"Have you taken leave of your senses?" he snapped.

"No," I replied coldly. "I am not asking you to come with me."

Bradley shook his head vigorously. "You're daft if you think I'm going to allow you to go alone."

Allow? Interesting choice of words. I was going, whether he came or not. Nothing was going to stop me. "Come then," I snapped.

Bradley indiscreetly rolled his eyes, presumably at the thought of marching back up those steps. There were less than one hundred stone steps leading up to the castle, but they were steep. And once you reached the top of those steps, you met the slight incline leading to the castle.

"Okay," he said, his voice betraying a hint of bitterness.

"Service with a smile, Bradley." Why did he put up with me? *Because he loved you*, a voice says. Loved. Past tense. Another knife in my heart.

Despite obvious efforts, he sniggered. "Let's go."

As we were leaving the inn, I shouted behind me, "Goodbye, George."

***

Walking out into the town which was cloaked in shadowy twilight, I heard George shout his goodbye. He will be dead now too.

The violent bruise-like colours of the sky only added to my already firmly established anxiety. And determination. Thoughts thundered through my mind: *Was this a good idea? Was it worth it? Was I right to take Bradley with me? Was this going to accomplish anything?*

Hindsight is a terrible thing. If I had known then what I know now, I never would have taken Bradley. Probably, I never would have gone myself, let alone carrying that blanket in my bag.

It was heavy and it obviously showed. "What is the matter with you?" Bradley asked mockingly, yet with a hint of concern.

I tried to avoid his worried glances, but couldn't. "I didn't tell you the whole plan," I said, heaving myself up the oversized hill. He rolled his eyes again. "Don't do that," I snapped. "You know me. I know what I'm doing."

Cruel irony.

"Well," he began reluctantly, "you can tell me now."

I told him how I aimed to spend the night in the library. If Lady Tabitha's ghost actually existed, she would appear. *Nothing else would happen*, I thought to myself. *Nothing else* could *happen. Ghosts can't hurt you. Not least of all because they don't exist.*

As the words left my mouth, I could almost feel him rolling his eyes. "I'm not understanding." Bradley was correct to be confused: after all, I sounded absurd. My entire idea was absurd. *Why* did I have to do that? If I hadn't, the ghost tour would never have happened. But, again, we are not there yet.

"You're not wise, Kathleen Mulligan," he said. I knew he wanted to argue with me about staying, to get out. But his unrelenting kindness stopped him.

The light diminished almost entirely by the time we had reached the castle. "Hope you remembered a lantern," Bradley said, sniggering. To his surprise, I pulled one out of my purse.

Without delay, I walked through the gates into the courtyard. An intense cold swept over me, a cold so bitter, I struggled to think properly. I know now

Lady Tabitha was watching me. A beast stalking its prey.

We worked our way over to the staff entrance which was a small door beside the kitchen: we knew where the key to that door was, or at least Bradley did, and I had an inkling.

In the gloomy night air, the wind whistled, making Bradley nervy. Every time he heard the slightest noise, he would swing around in a swift motion and whisper, "What was that?"

Every single time, I would tell him it was nothing, but nature. Of course, my thoughts echoed his and my anxiety doubled with each unexpected sound. *Was this a good idea? Was this wise?*

As I thought, Anne kept her keys under the flowerpot. I would usually have thought this was unsafe, but who would steal from a castle if you had to climb the Scottish equivalent of Mount Everest to get to it? Nobody.

An owl hooted, causing the two of us to jump in fright. Leaves crinkled in the wind. It was only half-past-eight, and already the town beneath us was immersed in an ocean of dark The world was sound asleep. There would be no moon that night.

We needn't have picked up the key: as we approached the door, it swung open.

As it opened, the hinges squealed in pain, or in warning?

My heartbeat sped up until its thumping was all I could hear or feel. Slowly, naively, stupidly, we walked over the threshold, leaving safety behind.

Inside, the cold deepened, plunging into my heart like a twisting knife. My breath formed a cloud in the light of my lantern.

"I'm sure the light switch is around here somewhere," Bradley said, his voice comforting me and also causing my heart to race, but for reasons other than fear. He stumbled around, knocking over just about every stool. "Ah, here it is."

My heart sped, pumping acidic blood through my body which corroded every part of me as I waited impatiently for Bradley to put on the gaslight. "What are you doing?" I unintentionally snapped.

"I can't," he answered shortly.

I shone my lantern in his direction as he was fumbling with the gaslight, but no light was forthcoming.

Even though I would never have admitted it at that time, I knew the light would not come.

"Apparently," Bradley said whimpering, his breath visible. "We've been to the castle; no ghost has appeared. Can we go please?"

Despite the fact that it was painfully obvious Bradley was terrified, I told him I was not leaving. I knew that if I stayed, he would as well. How selfish. I would leave him shaking in fear, just to pacify my own stubbornness.

"Why are we even here? What do you hope to achieve?" Bradley asked hurriedly, his emotions getting the better of him. His widened eyes, his shaking hands, his sweating brow. All of it is burned into my memory.

"Ghosts do not exist," I said decidedly. "I am here to prove it. Once and for all."

Sounds of the night echoed around us. The wind howled, sounding like satanic laughter. Nothing shook me more, however, than the crash that sounded from upstairs, followed by the most perilous scream anybody could have the misfortune to hear.

Bradley's expression plunged into fear like a pebble tossed into a rapid stream. His shaking was beyond belief. His mouth curved into an O as the gaslights switched themselves on.

"At least we have light now," I said in an attempt to calm his nerves, my own. My feeble attempt at levity did nothing to lessen my growing anxiety and it only heightened Bradley's.

Slowly, we edged our way out of the staff quarters. The second we had left it, my lantern began flickering. Even though deep in my heart I knew we were in the presence of something not-quite-human, my mind refused to believe it.

An odd sound reigned throughout the castle then. A sound I had not heard in a very long time: the laugh of my great-grandfather. He had passed away two years, three months and eleven days before at 11:40 p.m. Happily, if that is the right word to use, he died from old age. One-hundred-and-three. He had spent his life laughing and the sound of it brought happy, yet mournful, tears to my eyes. His laugh was soft and joyous.

I turned to Bradley who was looking around with more confusion than I had ever seen. When I twisted my head back, my grandfather stood before me, swaying in front of me to a tune I remembered vividly: the melody of my childhood music box.

It had a sweet sound, a beautiful tune. One I had fallen asleep listening to maybe a thousand times. Without realising it, I started to smile. The danger we were in had not even begun to cross my mind because of it, so, as we ventured further into the castle and further away from safety, but I couldn't say I wasn't feeling uneasy.

"Hello, Kathy," he said. If he had not been looking straight at me, I may have realised sooner that he was not actually there.

"Hello, Mully," I answered. I had always called him Mully: apparently when I first met him, I could not pronounce our last name properly; I said Mully all the time. Somehow, the nickname stuck with him. "I've missed you so much." As the words left my mouth, they sounded choked and bubbly. "I love you. We have been apart for too long and —"

"We have never been apart. I live on within your memory," Mully replied. "I never left you. I never will."

Mully opened his arms wide. I made to run into them, but Bradley grabbed my arm. "Who are you talking to?" he asked. I closed my eyes to let the tears out.

He was gone when I reopened them. At that moment, I began to reconsider the existence of ghosts: I was not convinced yet, however. "I thought I saw," I began, turning around to look again, just to make sure I *had* been imagining Mully. "Never mind that," I continued, pushing away the pain, blocking out the memories. "We need to get to the nursery."

Bradley's eyes fell upon me, betraying panic. "What is it?" I asked, every part of me beginning to regret bringing him with me. Although I would never have sent him back, the thought crossed my mind: his panic was not helping.

"I couldn't say," he replied, his teeth chattering. A frosty wind blew nonchalantly through the castle, causing my heart to send burning blood through me. "It felt like something had walked through me. Something dark, something after revenge. No love. Just hate."

Assuming his words were an attempt to frighten me more, I shouted, "Don't be ridiculous." How could anyone be angry with someone as loving, as kind, as generous, as gentle as Bradley?

Being the peacemaker he had always been, he said nothing in retaliation. I knew I had hurt him though. He would never do anything if he thought it might worsen a situation.

Every stair cried out in pain as we ascended. The wind screamed. I knew for a fact that they *never* made that sound normally. The castle had always been kept in perfect condition. All of it.

The lamplight reflected aggressively off the colossal windows on the first landing. Continuing to howl, the wind swept through McAvoy Castle.

"That was bright," Bradley said weakly, clearly still hurting after my comment. Why was I so cruel? I didn't mean to be; I didn't want to be. Especially not towards him.

"I don't remember a time when I could see properly," I said jokingly. He laughed feebly.

"I really do love you, Kathleen," he whispered. His words plunged into me like darts. I still remember the feeling. I still *feel* it. It was deep, insatiable. Yet another 'what if' moment.

"I know you do," I replied, abruptly ending the conversation.

I love you too, I wanted to scream.

The rest of the walk took what seemed like hours. Thuds resounded throughout the building, shrieks echoed. As we got closer to that room, they sounded more and more like excited squeals.

I stopped outside the library, knowing we were at the point of no return. If we went through, we would never be the same people again. If we didn't, we would be cowards. However, if we hadn't, Bradley would not have died.

We glanced at each other. "Are you ready?" he asked, taking my hand.

There was the sound of books being thrown across the library, a screaming woman's voice mingling with the sound of a shouting man. A cacophony of terror and unhappiness.

Heart pumping, I pushed open the door. Instantly, the lamp went out.

***

Hand in hand, coated in a soft purply light, we walked over the threshold. At once, Lord McAvoy's portrait began to swing, as did that of Lady Tabitha. Her eyes cut into me.

My breath clouded in front of me as cold swept over us.

Behind us, the fire ignited of its own volition, but adding nothing to the temperature. Demonic shadows flew around the room, shrouding us in an angry sea of black and orange.

Again, something breathed on the back of my neck. Refusing to turn around, too obstinate to face the demon, I tightened my grasp on Bradley's hand and we continued our walk to the nursery.

I'm not sure what it was, but something was enticing me, drawing me ever closer to the devil's domain. Something irresistible.

For some unfathomable reason, I thought it would be safe. The room of a child is usually the safest place in a home. That's the way it should be. My logic was flawed, however, as the McAvoy child died in that room.

Bradley's maddened breathing heightened my apprehension until all I could think about was getting out of there, getting home.

"*Why* are you so nervous?" I asked Bradley, feigning confidence. "We are not in danger."

He turned his head away from me, trying to hide tears.

"Bradley," I said, grimacing at the false condescension in my voice, "there are no such things as ghosts. We are safe."

Satanic laughter ricocheted. A strange groaning erupted out of Bradley, a hysterical whimper. All I could think about was getting home, getting Bradley home. "Do you want to leave?" I asked, trying to sound irritated.

The truth is, I wanted to run. I did not want to show fear, though. I refused to betray my own nerves.

Why did I bring him? *Why*?

Bradley merely nodded in response. My Bradley. I *miss* him. So much it hurts.

We turned to leave. A vicious gust of wind extinguished the fire's flames. "See," I said, nudging him gently. "There is *nothing* to be afraid of. It's dark, we're in an old castle. Our imaginations are going wild. We are in no danger." I could hear the doubt edging into my voice, but I refused to let Bradley notice.

We walked out of the library. A cruel laugh reigned over McAvoy's estate as we marched down the steps. We stopped dead. "It's the wind," I whispered unconvincingly. "That's all."

That's all I would let it be.

Bradley didn't stop though and dragged me along the corridor. "*Why* did you want to come here?" he asked, his chest heaving, his voice shaking. "Why?"

"To prove there's no ghost," I replied simply.

"How is that going for you?"

"Very well."

"How do you explain the fire igniting?" he snapped, picking up speed.

"It obviously wasn't put out properly." Again, every step cried out in anguish under our weight.

Without even looking at me, Bradley shook his head. "Kathleen, the fire is never lit. We are not allowed to light it."

We reached the ground floor and galloped across to the door, our footsteps echoing in the darkness. My hair stood on end as unknown eyes fell on me. Without slowing down, I turned my head.

No. Impossible. Ghosts do not *exist.* I opened my mouth to scream, but stopped myself. "Lady Tabitha is *dead*. She's gone." *You're just tired*, I told myself. Before I could look again, to hopefully validate my so-called irrational fear, we were in the courtyard.

I had no idea that I had just received another warning. My final warning.

If I had just accepted the truth, they would still be alive. I failed. I failed them all.

Now that we were outside, Bradley let out a small, relieved giggle. "Never thought I would be in McAvoy Castle at night," he told me while we ran down the hill, heading into the village. "I never believed the stories growing up. How wrong was I?"

I furrowed my eyebrows, searching my memory. "What are you talking about?" I asked, my words barely audible through my hastened breathing.

"Stories my grandfather used to tell me. Basically, the ghost of Lady Tabitha stalks the castle at night, waiting for the first girl of one who wronged her, longing for revenge, waiting. I'm glad I'm not the one who wronged her."

I allowed myself to smile, apparently forgetting the fact that her crimson ghost had looked directly at me. I mean, I couldn't have been the one to wrong her! I wasn't even born until decades after she died. It's impossible that I could've wronged her. Unless —

No, I chastised myself. *Don't be ridiculous. It couldn't have anything to do with him. No. That's absurd.*

We arrived back in the village, said our 'goodnights' and headed home. All the way, I repeated myself about how ridiculous my thought had been. It *was* absurd …

***

I woke the next morning, after a broken sleep. After dressing, I headed straight to the castle: despite my restless night, I'd slept in. Work started at nine. In fifteen minutes.

Walking speedily up to the dominion of death, I smirked at my apparent immaturity. *How,* I wondered, *could I have been so addled to think I'd seen a ghost?*

When I finally reached the castle, Anne was standing in the courtyard, shivering. "Morning, Anne," I chirped. "How are you? Why are you standing out here?"

She looked at me through frozen eyes. "Morning, Kathleen," she replied, her teeth chattering manically. "Malcolm wants to see us all in the staff quarters."

Too tired to ask why and not being particularly interested in the answer anyway, I dawdled along to the meeting. As I walked through the colossal wooden doors, the overwhelming cold crept back into me though. Although I didn't believe it, chills ran down my spine as I walked passed one of Lady Tabitha's portraits. Once more, hateful eyes watched my every move. I refused to look up.

It was just my imagination.

Strolling into the staff quarters was like walking into the Head's Office at school: you always knew it was important and *every* wrong thing you'd ever done ran through your mind.

Everybody was looking at me, almost searchingly. I've always been self-conscious. Therefore, I seated myself down on the chair nearest to the back wall. I endeavoured not to catch anyone's eye, especially the unearthly apparition at the door, which was pointing directly at me. "What do you want with me?" I screamed.

Everybody's eyes were on me.

"Let's not shout at the ghosts, Kathleen," Malcolm snapped.

"So, you saw it too?" I asked, before realising the intent behind his abrasion. I ignored it though, but I couldn't avoid the terrified glances Anne and Harold exchanged.

"There are no ghosts, child. Leave the dead in their graves." Malcolm spoke with so much venom that it was unsettling. "Ridiculous child," he muttered.

Bradley leapt to his feet ferociously, sending his chair flying. "If we're done," he hissed, "perhaps you'd be kind enough to tell us why we're here when we should be working."

Studiously *not* looking at Lady Tabitha, I focused on Bradley. His rage was clear, but his intentions now moves me to tears: he risked losing his position at the castle to defend my honour. He was so loving. So gentle. So young. *Too* young.

"Sit down," Malcolm boomed. "You're like a lovesick puppy. It's repugnant. She *clearly* doesn't love you back, so move on with your life, lad. Anyway, one of you," he continued, scanning the room, "came here last night and I want to know who. And why."

"It was me," I said immediately. "I forgot my bag, so came back to get it." In response, Malcolm nodded while sauntering to the far wall and picking something up. My lantern … I must've dropped it. He didn't say a word. Perhaps that would've been better. He just looked at me through analytical, merciless eyes.

"I came to disprove the existence of ghosts," I said, mortified. "Something happened in the nursery."

"Disprove the existence of ghosts?" he gasped. "I suppose you wanted to have an adventure. For *goodness* sake, leave the dead in their grave. Lady Tabitha is nothing more than bones in a box. Her daughter is dead. Her husband is dead. That's that. End of story. Learn to live in the real world."

Losing the battle, I moved my eyes to look at the ghost.

Furious retorts sped through my head. Employing a hitherto unseen amount of energy, I restrained myself. There's no point arguing with people who won't listen, who won't try to understand.

He rushed from the room.

Lady Tabitha, red as fury, smiled venomously before stalking after him.

Clinging to my obstinacy, to my long held disbelief in ghosts, I turned to Anne: she had worked at the castle longer than anyone. If it *was* haunted, she would know. More than that, Anne would tell the truth.

When I asked her, all colour drained from her face. She looked at me with an expression I *still* can't describe … worried? Despaired? Pitying?

Taking my hand and wrapping it in hers, she stood and led me outside, whipped out a pipe and puffed away. Anne must have seen the confusion on across my face. "My pipe is for emergencies," she told me. "It was my husband's." Taking a deep breath, she continued, "There is a ghost here. You must know the story," she said.

I nodded. "None of us are in any danger. However, do *not* come here at night. Especially not now." I shot her a quizzical look. "Tomorrow marks the anniversary of her miscarriage."

I nodded again, comprehending. "What has that got to do with me?"

"Nothing." She spoke a little too loudly to convince me. Not to mention, she sounded *off* … like she was trying to convince herself. "Nothing at all," she whispered.

Raising an eyebrow at her, I repeated my question. "Honesty, please, Anne. She watches me. I can feel her eyes on me now."

Before Anne could answer, an unnatural grotesque *crunch* sounded. "What was that?" I gasped.

My blood chilled as I What had she done to him? *You're being ridiculous*, I told myself, going to find him. He'd be around somewhere. *So what was the crunch?* I diligently ignored the voice from within me, the voice telling me to run, to get as far away as I could.

A shadow obscured my view of the grandfather clock, but not enough to hide the black feather from view. Above the feather, swinging from the bannister was Malcolm, a look of petrified surrender carved into his face. Malcolm's eyes, lifeless and traumatised by whatever he had seen, stared directly at me.

His mouth hung open, silently screaming. All colour had drained out of him. Paler than a porcelain doll, he hung.

I couldn't scream. Believe me, I wanted to. I longed to scream until all the air had flooded out of me. Above his swinging corpse stood Lady Tabitha, a triumphant, gleeful smirk resting on her face. I blinked, and she was gone.

She's real.

I can't even begin to articulate what was going through my mind.

She's real. Not only that, she's lethal.

Anne's wail pierced my brain. I still hear it at night. A wave of high-pitched, anguished squeals sucked all the life from McAvoy Castle.

***

Police closed McAvoy Castle while they carried out necessary investigations. Having declared Malcolm's death as a suicide, they reopened it a week later.

In deference to Anne's wishes – who I know knew Lady Tabitha had something to do with Malcolm's death – I didn't tell the officers about the feathers, about what I'd seen.

I will never forgive myself for Malcolm's death, or any of the others. I won't ask God for forgiveness either: I don't deserve it. I don't have the courage to ask for it.

How did Lady Tabitha make Malcolm do it? He was happy! Well, maybe 'happy' isn't the right word, but he would never have killed himself. Ever. He cared too much about himself. I know it sounds harsh, but it's true.

All residents of our little town attended his funeral. Nobody in the community particularly cared for him while he was alive. It's harrowing, but he was *not* a kind person. People care much more when you're dead. No family attended. Nobody could locate them. Malcolm both lived and died alone.

Standing at the graveside, I couldn't help but feel responsible. If I'd warned him about the ghost, would he still be alive now? If I had, would he have believed me?

We assembled by the grave, under the shadow of the castle. Lady Tabitha was watching us. I know it.

"We commit his body to the ground, earth to earth, ashes to ashes, dust to dust."

***

Seven days later, McAvoy's estate re-opened for the staff. None of us wanted to return. Especially not Anne.

She was feeling unwell since Malcolm died. I greatly admired her for braving the castle again.

Before I was born, her son killed himself by hanging. I think that's why she believed in ghosts. It wasn't through choice, but through need. People tend not to believe in things that scare them to the point of denial. Anne needed ghosts to be real so she could feel her son still being close to her. He was only seventeen. And he loved that castle, which is why she stayed.

When I saw how unhappy, how *empty* she looked, I told her to take a walk by the loch. Taking a stroll by Scotland's waters always soothed me as a child, making anxiety give way to serenity.

I was back in the nursery, cleaning with Bradley. Well, Bradley was cleaning. I was staring out the window, watching Anne, feeling unbearably helpless. Although I still clung to a modicum of doubt in my mind about the ghost, I would not go into that room alone.

It was freezing in the nursery. My breath clouded in front of me, steaming up the window.

I watched Anne, trying to think of something – anything – to speak about with Bradley … something other than the obvious. Anne walked speedily, probably to keep warm, whilst gazing at the water.

I wish I knew what she was thinking: I can speculate, of course. But I'll never know. Why did I send her out alone? Another addition to my long list of regrets. My life is a long list of regrets.

"Kathleen," Bradley began, "you can't blame yourself for … you know."

"How do you know I am?"

"Because I know you. I saw the way you were at the funeral. You were the only one crying. I know the expression you wear when you feel responsible for something. You've worn it since he died." He walked over to the window and looked at me. "You're wearing it now."

A breeze brushed against the back of my neck. I spun around, expecting to see the hellish red glow. I didn't. An eerie chill flowed through my body, freezing me from the inside out. I stepped off the window ledge, tripped over something and fell onto the crib.

Immediately, fire replaced chill, burning through me. Anguished cries exploded in my throat, erupted out of me.

Bradley knelt next to me, wrapping me in his arms. "What's wrong?" he cried. "Kathleen!"

I flung my arm out to point at the window. Through agony, I squeezed my eyes shut, gritted my teeth. *Stop screaming*, I told myself. Bradley hovered over me, his eyes haunted.

"Check on Anne!" I forced the words out through my teeth, so they were little more than tortured groans.

Miraculously, he understood and stumbled over to the window.

Please, I prayed. *Please let her be safe and well.* Bradley's face drained. His eyes widened and his chest heaved. "She's not there …"

I forced myself to my feet, endeavouring to quell the fire raging through me. I didn't waste time looking out of the window. Instead, I bulleted through and out of McAvoy Castle. The cold was unrelenting. Never had I experienced a wintry chill of such intensity.

Bradley was following me closely and, by the time I reached the loch, Harold had caught up. "What on earth is going on?" he asked, his face contorted with confusion and worry.

Regardless of the bitter frost whitening the grounds, regardless of the icy wind, I was going to save her. I don't know how, but I knew Lady Tabitha had made her fall in. I didn't even know where exactly she had landed in the loch, but I was going to save her. I *was*. I *was*.

"What," Harold continued, "in the name of sanity is going on?"

The surface bubbled. Anne was still alive!

I briefly explained to Harold, while taking my shoes off. "I'm going in."

"Don't be ridiculous," Harold spluttered. "You will die."

I panted, the cold already cutting through me, "If I don't, she will."

I ran to the water. Bradley grabbed me. He pulled me back. I screamed and screamed, and screamed, spewing every heinous word I knew. He was too strong. I couldn't move. All I could do was squirm and wriggle. "Get off me," I screeched. "Please!"

I don't remember anything else I said. I was probably incoherent.

My heart was breaking. It shatters every time I think the photograph of the castle's staff.

I'm not in the main photograph: it was taken about six months before I joined. They're all there though. They are all smiling.

It's been ten years. Ten years since it all ended. Every time the anniversary comes, I just cry. I can't stop it. I don't try. Every year, my throat closes up, but, for the rest of the world, it's just another day. They've forgotten. Everybody has moved on. Everybody except me. *Time heals*, they say. Time does not make things easier. People just learn to live with the emptiness in their hearts.

Every time I think of that wonderful photograph, I'm reminded of the days we spent together and a brief spell of happiness follows. Until I'm plagued with the memory that there were supposed to be so many more days. Thousands of days that we never spent together. I have nothing left. Nothing but days of emptiness. Bradley. Anne. Malcolm. Harold. All of them ... gone.

Why was *I* the one to survive? Why didn't she just kill me?

***

I can't remember what happened after that. My memory clarifies three hours later, when I, once again, was sprawled across the chaise longue.

My eyes stung with dried tears. I couldn't move; I was immobilised by the weight of my conscience.

Anne was – was gone. Forever. I would never speak to her again. I would never see her again. She would never breathe again. Because of me. Because of my obstinacy and arrogance.

Why did I feel as if I knew everything? "*Go for a walk by the water,*" I said. If I'd just minded my own business, she'd still be alive today. But she's not: she's dead. Because of me.

Harold rushed into the room, his face riddled with indecision, misshapen by grief and pain.

I knew what needed to be done. Thinking about it, it was quite clear that the demon was after me. No-one else. Unless she was killing people to get at me.

"Anne's body hasn't been found yet," Harold whimpered as he sat down next to me. "The police have left. They couldn't find her. They won't be back today. I'm not going to ask you how you feel because I already know."

You really have no idea, I thought to myself. How could he possibly understand? Without me, none of this would've happened. I started this, so it was up to me to end it. Alone.

Malcolm and Anne, who had their lives torn from them before their time was up, called to me from wherever they were. They demanded my resistance. They commanded me to be strong. For them. For myself. I knew in that moment that I was going to come back to the castle alone. I was going to face the devil myself.

I knew – well, thought I knew – that I was going to die. But, I didn't care. I anticipated death. I longed for death.

Before I joined the staff at that castle, energy had surged through me. Life poured out of me. I loved everything about my existence. It was perfect.

I miss living now. I breathe, I don't live.

Lady Tabitha took my life and emptied it. She ripped everyone I loved away from me. I will be alone. Forever.

Finally, in that moment, I believed unconditionally that it was time for me to face my demon and end the line of corpses with my own.

I looked around the room, hating everything I used to adore.

Never would I look at that place the same way again. Burning fury filled me.

"This is all my fault," I told Harold. I was about to lay my soul completely bare, tell him everything. Explain how Lady Tabitha had targeted me for some unknown reason, but I stopped. Would telling him lead to unanswerable questions?

Why, he might have asked, *is Lady Tabitha after you and you alone? What would make you the subject of her hatred?*

Would he even believe me? It was my duty, my obligation, to let someone know though. "I … I …," was all I managed.

"This castle is closed until further notice. More than likely, it'll never open to the public again." There was something – something remorseful in his tone. I knew he was regretting something, but trying to hide it from me. "He should have let this place be forgotten."

A few years before I was born, McAvoy Castle was losing its popularity. Closure seemed inevitable. Unavoidable. However, since Malcolm's stubbornness matched my own and, because he rejected failure to the point of lunacy, he had poured money into keeping it open. Never was his contribution allowed to be forgotten.

"I know," I replied. It was all I could say. Nothing could distract me from the eternal depths of indecision clouding his eyes. I could tell he wanted to tell me something, but was endeavouring to restrain himself. He had never been particularly skilled in talking. I still don't understand why he tried.

Having spent several hundred hours of my life trying to figure out his reasons, I've now given up. Another addition to my never-ending list of unanswered questions.

"What are you hiding?" I asked.

"I don't think – " he began.

"No. Don't do that," I hissed, pushing myself up to a sitting position. "Tell me." I couldn't care less about the aggression suddenly erupting out of me. I still don't.

"We've always known about Lady Tabitha. Nobody would believe us if we told them, so we've always steered people away from their suspicions."

"How many lives," I started, my words drowned out by the now howling wind. "How many people have you lied to?"

Harold could do nothing, but look at the rug. Tears wettened his cheeks. "I'm sorry."

It was in that moment I understood why Harold had always been so shy. It was to stop himself from telling untruths.

He wanted to help people.

"We could've saved them!" I boomed. "There's nothing more tragic than a preventable death."

Then the red mist of rage overwhelmed me. I want you, reader, to understand why I exploded, releasing all my built-up fury and guilt: I didn't want him to follow me. It was not to hurt him.

I knew I would return that night. I wasn't going to take any chances of anyone coming after me.

***

I sat idly in my room, staring, unblinking, at the castle, waiting for all lights to go out.

Finally, they did. After waiting a while, I grabbed my bag, threw a lantern into it and slung it onto my back.

My eyes watering, my hands shaking as I edged closer and closer to hysteria, I slid the key into the lock of my family's front door and left.

My legs pulled me to McAvoy Castle. Before I had time to formulate any sort of plan, I was standing in the courtyard, illuminated by the moon. A vile cold buried itself in my body and I knew she was watching me. Fear had no hold on me. Determination thwarted its control. The nondescript door creaked open.

"Here we go," I muttered. Just as I was about to walk in, I turned around to take one final look at the village I'd loved and called home. "I'm sorry."

I grew up here. I thought nostalgically of all the wonderful days I spent there as a child. In spite of everything that had happened, I was sorry to leave. All of my past mistakes eroded the happy memories and relentless grief seeped into me.

Bradley. Bradley.

"It's time to do the right thing," I said to myself. All I was hoping was that my death would be quick.

I walked over the threshold, my heart pumping. *Don't be scared*, I told myself.

***

The temperature fell like a boulder off a cliff as I set foot inside the castle. The spirit's painfully frosty stare fell upon me. Creaking – the unsettling, yet familiar creaking – sounded from upstairs.

"This ends now, Tabitha!" I screeched, marching up the stairs, awaiting the arrival of Cu Sith.

I didn't fear anything other than failing to do the right thing. Life is not measured by how much you achieve, but how many you help.

Despair seized me, however. Tears filled my eyes and my heart raced. In spite of the plummeting temperature, I was dripping with perspiration.

I reached the top of that once beautiful staircase and the creaking intensified, growing louder, louder, louder.

It was coming from the library. No, the nursery. No, the bedroom behind me. No, the evening living room. No … she was toying with me, trying to see how long I would last before I ran home.

She wanted to see me quiver with trepidation, to surrender. When she killed Anne, however, she killed my fear and gave life to my rage. My fear lay at the bottom of the loch alongside Anne. I would *not* run this time. I would not show any emotion.

I swerved at the sound of a rattling door handle. It came from the bedroom, from inside. It was almost always locked. I couldn't remember the last time it had been open.

She thinks that's going to scare me, I thought, a defiant grin forming on my face. "I'm not scared anymore. You have killed too many. It's time to end this, demon."

I kicked the door and it flew open.

No. Please, no.

"I told you she'd come," Bradley said, turning his head to the shadow behind him. Harold. Bradley's tone was incredulous. The look on his face screamed, "*We need to leave.*"

"Get out!" I screamed, all emotion pouring out of me. "It's not safe! GET OUT!"

I couldn't save them, I knew that, but I had to try. "GET OUT!" I bellowed, storming back down the stairs, hoping against all the odds they would leave.

Thundering through the castle, I couldn't shake the feeling that we were being followed.

"Please, Bradley," I said, refusing to turn around, to let him see my face. "Please go home."

"I'm not going anywhere without you." He paused, no doubt noticing the ominous glow in the kitchen, shining under the gap of the door. Pounding footsteps approached us from behind. I didn't need to look to know it was Harold: his heavy footfall was unmistakable.

The shimmering intensified. Bradley took my hand. His pulse hammered in his skin, sweat moistened his palm. His hurried, shallow breathing … his attempt at feigning fearlessness … I remember it *too* vividly. The memory drains my soul, ossifies my blood.

I'm going to need to go in there, I thought. I wanted more time with Bradley, despite knowing all I'd bring him is pain. I didn't want to let go of his hand. *It's your duty*, I reminded myself.

"I'll go," Harold stated as if he'd read my mind. Bradley's hand fell away from mine. Forever. My eyes filling with tears – guilty tears – I begged him not to do this.

To my shock and confusion, Harold's lips curved into a smile. A grateful smile. "I've nothing to lose. Your friendship ... all of the friendships I've enjoyed while working here have made my life worth living. They've shown me the truth: life is truly meaningless when spent without the people who make you happy. My life has been largely solitary. I've lived my life without any relatives." His voice shook. "I can't remember my family, but this family of friends is worth risking everything to save. Thank you for bringing out the best in me."

Without saying another word, Harold passed me and bravely marched into the kitchen.

He then chortled. "We're well and truly daft. It's the light of the moon. Nothing else." His cheery and relieved tone did nothing to quell my internal disquietude.

He turned to leave the kitchen, but the door slammed with an almighty crash. *Click.*

His screams. Agonised. Tortured. Anguished.

I ran to the door, pounding it with my fists, booming his name with all the power in my vocal chords. His cries continued, unhindered. Unfiltered.

Slowly, very slowly, *painfully* slowly, the door slid open. I bolted in.

"Harold," I said, gasping. Nothing. I was cloaked in darkness.

"Bradley," I said, weeping, knowing Harold was gone. "Find candles!

"I will!" he called back.

Then the lamps came to life, temporarily blinding me with their intense brightness.

Harold was gone. In his place, lying on the cold stone floor, was a photograph of my great-grandfather … *What?* Why is – why would …? I bent down and picked it up. Sure enough, it was him. My incredibly kind, loving, God-fearing Mully. Despite the circumstances, I couldn't help but smile as I thought of him: there is nothing so powerful as memory.

And all my memories of that man are joyous. He was the kindest, most generous and hard-working man I have ever met and ever will meet. Lady Tabitha had made a mistake: Mully kept me fighting.

Nothing would stop me now. "This ends tonight," I screamed, causing Bradley to glare at me.

Without realising, I turned the photograph in my hand. On the back, written in Mully's gorgeous, calligraphic handwriting were the words:

The day I was appointed as doctor to the McAvoy family.

"Bradley," I whimpered, "I know why she is doing this." My strangled words still pain my heart. He didn't respond, except with a confused glance.

"Lady Tabitha's child was a little girl. My great-grandfather was their doctor." My love's perplexity deepened. "You said she wanted revenge on the first girl of the one who wronged her."

"I don't under —"

"I am the first female descendant of Mully."

Without a moment's hesitation, he took hold of my hand. "We have to get out of here."

I agreed simply to get Bradley away from her. We dashed for the nearest exit. Laughter rained down. The door slammed, locked, followed by a cacophony of thuds as every chance of escape was taken.

We were trapped.

Whoosh!

We swung around to see an orange flickering coming from upstairs.

The library.

I held the photograph of my heroic great-grandfather tenaciously. *With his memory, I'll be brave,* I told myself. I rushed upstairs.

Bradley ran up the stairs after me.

We were outside the library.

***

We walked over the threshold. Why was I so stubborn? I had had countless warnings, copious opportunities to get out of that condemned place, infinite chances to tell Bradley I loved him. I had thwarted any hope of happiness I once had and I didn't even know it. Such is the price of obstinacy.

The sound of a door locking stung my ears. We were trapped. "Well," I whispered to Bradley, "there's no way out now. If we die —"

"Don't say that. Please."

"If we die, I am glad my last moments have been spent with you."

Cold ossified my blood and I knew we were in the presence of something not quite human. My hand started to tingle as we were dragged towards the nursery.

Bradley interlocked his fingers in mine. The lamplight flickered.

"What is happening?" Bradley cried, the child in him clearly wanting to run away to safety. His voice was followed by a tremendous sound, almost like an explosion.

"I don't know," I snapped. Static electricity ran through my hand and the flickering lamp fell to the ground, its glass shattering. Once again, we were drenched in darkness.

"*Ring-a-ring o' roses.*"

A child's music box. The sound was distorted, slower than it should be, echoing around us.

Swish.

I swung my body round, but saw nothing.

Swish. I turned again and still saw nothing.

"Bradley?" I whispered, turning to look at him.

The nursery candelabra lit itself. My sight came back in splinters.

Bradley was not there. My hands were interlocked with themselves, not his. *Where* was Bradley?

I screamed his name.

"*A pocket full of posies.*"

"BRADLEY!" I tried to scream again, but no sound left my mouth.

"A-tishoo! A-tishoo!"

All I could hear was that child's music box. Then, a new voice. A dark voice, betraying enjoyment. "Come through, dearie."

I fought to get away, but my legs continued moving forward. Salty tears filled my eyes as I tried to scream again.

What was happening?

Another explosive thump, this time further away. Another. Another.

The dragging recommenced.

"We all fall down."

An extraordinarily strong wind hurled me onto the far wall of the nursery. My head smashed a painting and I was showered with broken wood.

"Wha-What?" I stuttered. That's not possible. BANG. BANG. BANG.

My pulse raced, thumped in my throat. The curtains swayed angrily. The wind howled.

BANG. BANG. BANG.

"BRADLEY!" I screamed. Vulnerable. Defenceless. Alone.

"KATH—," he screeched. The door to the nursery cried out in pain as it opened. Icy frost coated the windows. The curtains fell silent. Motionless.

BANG. BANG. BANG.

"BRADLEY!"

Where was he? What was he doing? What was happening to him?

"BRADLEY!" I screamed. A terrible wail echoed throughout the castle.

My vision blurred …

A heavily pregnant Lady Tabitha walked gleefully into the nursery. Her radiant joy filled the room. My guess was that she was in her sixth month.

She carried a bundle of children's books, tied together with a purple ribbon. Her shining smile warmed my heart, but also cooled my blood.

She gently placed the books on an intricately decorated oak cabinet and turned to leave. Her pretty holly-green glow flickered and her face contorted as she stumbled black, an ocean of crimson spilling over her exquisite dress.

"HELP! SOMEBODY PLEASE HELP MY BABY!"

Thundering footsteps sounded, coming nearer and nearer. A man – who I recognised instantly as Lord Earl McAvoy – shot into the room.

"Doctor!" he screamed, his voice tortured.

The Mully ran in … he tried and tried and tried. His endeavours failed. He couldn't save the baby.

The blur vanished. I scrambled to my feet and rushed for the door.

A monstrous cackle engulfed the estate.

"BRADLEY!" I cried.

No answer. I grabbed the door handle and tugged. *Please,* I begged silently, *please.* Still, the door refused to budge.

I was alone in the nursery again. Tears coursed down my cheeks.

"BRADLEY!" I screamed.

Shadows flew around the room.

"Why are you doing this?" I cried, my voice torn by fear. "Please let him go. Please." Another feather fell to my feet. Another. Another.

Bradley screamed again.

It's all my fault. It's all my fault. It's *all* my fault!

Why did I have to bring him back to that castle? Why did I take him? *Why* didn't I just leave things? Simply because I was too stubborn.

Creak ... Creak ...

Bradley screamed my name, begged to leave. As he screamed, the door *finally* opened. I sprinted through the library.

The fire roared and cackled. But I didn't care enough to stop. In fact, I sped up, ignoring the swinging portrait. All I wanted to do was get the two of us out of that demonic building and never return.

"Bradley!" I boomed, hoping desperately to be heard over the howling wind which clattered against the aged windows, causing them to cry out in pain. One shattered as an upstairs door crashed open.

Rain cascaded off the battlements. Bradley cried my name. *What* was he doing up there? I silently prayed for our escape as I stomped up the steps onto the roof. Rain stabbed me all over, but a warm relief poured through me when I saw Bradley.

I yelled his name and ran over to him. *We will get away,* I remember thinking. If only *we* did.

As I got closer, a red, glowing figure appeared behind him, hovering over the battlement.

Lady Tabitha. She laughed as she did it. She smirked as I begged her not to kill him, as I pleaded with her to let the boy I loved go.

My heart is burning …

The crimson demon flew through the love of my life and vanished. His eyes were lifeless as he fell over the edge.

***

So there you have it. That's it. They were all gone, my love was gone, my life was gone. Nothing remained.

Now, as death comes for me, I welcome it. I have told my story. Their deaths are explained.

Their graves remain unmarked. As I hope mine will.

The Screaming Woman

Dedicated to my secondary school English teachers. Thank you for your patience, and your   belief.

Grant Hopkins' alarm blared at seven o'clock on his first day as sheriff of Cathburn. He had studied diligently through his school years for this moment, this job. An electric current buzzed through him as he thought of putting on that golden badge. The star of honour was, in his opinion, greater than any medal anyone could ever earn. It was what he had always dreamed of doing: protecting the streets of his town. Nothing, he thought, could make him prouder.

Having grown up in Cathburn, Grant had watched his mother's cousin, Maxwell Carter, protecting the streets of America. He remembered thinking how perfectly brave Maxwell was. He was his hero, his role model. The man he had spoken to before buying the engagement ring with which he was going to propose to Emily Wilton.

Kind, intelligent, loving, generous, compassionate, gorgeous. With every fibre of his being, Grant adored her. Everyone in Cathburn did. Who wouldn't? She never had a harsh word to say about anyone, or anything. Emily's love for people could never be matched. Not by anyone Grant knew. She had time for everyone and anyone.

Grant remembered moving to Cathburn when his parents divorced. Aged five, Emily had been the first to introduce herself. She was first friend.

He opened the box, gazing at the beautiful flower comprised of a ruby surrounded by diamonds, sitting atop a silver ring. Smiling, Grant slipped it into his pocket.

"Tonight," he whispered to himself, unable to stop smiling.

On his way to work he went over how he would ask the girl he loved to be his wife.

Two decades had passed. In the following years, they had participated in many charity events. After all, that is what Emily and Grant cared about the most: helping others.

Walking along Main Street, Grant went over his proposal plan: he would take Emily to her favorite restaurant. She simply revered the food made at Ava Black. It wasn't his kind of food: it was too ... too *different*.

Not that it mattered: his aim for tonight, and for the rest of their lives, was to keep Emily happy. Everything would be perfect. Grant would reserve 'Emily's table' – the one overlooking the highway.

Emily would sit and watch all the cars go by, commenting on all the different lives passing them by. All the different stories.

Grant's smile shone as he thought of the song he would ask the restaurant to play as they sipped on champagne: *I Do It For You*. It was to be the perfect evening, a perfect end to the perfect day.

"Morning," Mr. MacMillan, the local hotel owner, said as Grant passed the door, pulling him out of his thoughts. "First day in the new job? Good luck!"

Grant replied, "Thank you, Major."

It had been a running joke for many years: Mr MacMillan had fought in the American army during the Second World War. Jokingly, he instructed Grant to call him 'Major whenever he saw him. Aged eighty-nine, he vowed never to retire. *Retirement*, he always said, *leads to a lack of discipline*.

Chuckling, the pair parted ways.

"Good luck today, pal," George Waterson, Cathburn's chief accountant said in passing. Cathburn actually only had one accountant, one sheriff, and one lawyer. It wasn't big enough to need more.

As Grant marched ecstatically towards the Sheriff's Office, several people wished him good luck on his first day.

Birds nesting upon the sheriff's office roof greeted Grant with a beautiful song. "I will protect this town. I will protect these people." Grant paused, turning to look around. "Not that there is anything around here to protect them from," he murmured.

Cathburn had the lowest crime rate in the United States and every resident was proud of their town's reputation. Tourism didn't bring a lot of money, but when people came, they returned, commenting on how safe they felt. Never had there been any malice in Cathburn. That's why Grant and his family had moved there.

Delightedly, he pushed open the office doors. The smell of liquorice and smoke filled his nostrils, bringing nostalgia as he thought of the days he'd spent with Maxwell, his mother's cousin and his best friend in this office.

Grant walked to the desk, switched on the computer, made himself a steaming cup of coffee and phoned Ava Black's restaurant to make sure everything was ready.

He placed a photograph of his magnificent girlfriend on the left side of the computer and his parents on the right side. In the middle lay his badge.

"Good morning, Ava Black's, how may I help?" someone chirped. *A man,* Grant knew. *New to the job.* It was obvious: employees at Ava Black were not known for their enthusiasm.

"Hi, hello," Grant began. "I reserved a table for seven o'clock. The one overlooking the highway. I was wondering if everything is ready? The name is Hopkins. It's for the proposal."

"Sure thing. Hold on, sir, and I'll check."

"Thank you."

"Of course, sir," the enthusiastic employee replied. A minute or so passed before the man returned. "Everything is ready, sir." Grant's lips curved at the edges as he heard the words.

"I wish you the very best. We will see you at seven."

"Thank you very much," Grant said, before hanging up.

Shaking with electric excitement, Grant reached for his golden star, which was glittering in the sunlight. Unable to stop smiling, he opened the badge, slipped it into his shirt and he closed the safety pin.

It was *finally* official: he was now sheriff of Cathburn, protector of the vulnerable. He was proud, honoured, blessed.

***

Grant took a sip from his second cup of coffee and was gazing lovingly at the photograph of Emily when, all at once, his tranquillity vanished. He could not believe it when a scream reverberated around the small town. Grant had never heard anything like it before. It was a mixture of terror and shock. The scream of a woman. A petrified woman.

Grant shot out of the office, almost being struck down by the sun's heat. The screams sounded louder.

Grant saw her instantly. Running like a frightened gazelle up Main Street. Cloaked in blood, she hurtled straight towards him.

People attempted to aid her; but she pushed them away, her screaming growing louder. George tried to grab her and calm her down. With one swift motion, she kicked him and he fell away. The rest of the townsfolk retreated with him.

But it was now Grant's turn to be the sheriff.

She was running toward him again.

"HELP!" she screeched, her deranged voice terrifying Grant. "SOMEONE HELP ME! PLEASE!" she bellowed, galloping ever closer to the sheriff's office.

Grant stood there, unable to move, though he longed to.

Though Grant could not explain why, there was something within his very core telling him to run, telling him Cathburn's safety would soon be threatened.

Who was this woman? What had she experienced? Why was she trying to push them all away, even as she'd clearly come there for help?

Whatever he felt, he knew his job meant he must serve and protect. Those words summed up not only his job, but his life's ambition. He *had* to do something.

The woman shook and clasped her hair with her hands.

"HELP!" she screeched again. "P-P-PLEASE!"

The screaming woman then started to writhe as though having a seizure. Her psychotic shrieking intensified and Grant just managed to get a hold of her as she fell into his arms.

***

Five minutes passed before the screaming woman could speak. Even then, her words weren't coherent.

"Poor, poor woman," Grant murmured. "I have never seen so much terror."

Pacing, he searched his brain in desperate hope that he'd think of the right thing to do.

She opened her maddened eyes and started to quake again.

Sitting bolt upright, she scanned Grant's office, taking everything in.

"Where am I?" she stuttered. "How did I get here?"

Grant sat next to her and consolingly said, "It's all right, miss. You passed out in the street. I carried you in." She looked at him through uncomforted eyes. "You're safe now."

The woman shook her head. "Body. There's a body in the woods." Sweat dripped from her wild hair onto her face.

"Body?" Grant gasped. This was not the first day he had bet on having. "What body? What are you talking about?"

Panic threatened, but he refused to let it dominate his thoughts. *I'm the sheriff now*, he reminded himself.

With melancholy, he looked at the map of Cathburn, sitting peacefully on the opposite wall. He had grown up there. The worst thing that had ever happened was a petty assault … Never had a body been involved. No-one died in Cathburn. Ever. Nobody to his knowledge had ever actually died in Cathburn. They went away to do it.

Nothing could have prepared him for this day. But he knew what he had to do. Protect and serve his community. To do that, he would go to the woods, following the woman's lead to find the body. How could this be happening?

Could he take her back there though? Heck, the entire town had seen, and heard, the state she was in. But he had to. The woods were deep and he might never find the corpse otherwise.

"I'm sorry," he began, "you need to show me where the body is." He tried in vain to speak gently.

She looked up at him through menaced eyes. A moment passed and she nodded.

***

Sheriff Hopkins' car smelt like liquorice and smoke so Grant knew *Maxwell must have been in here.* Driving toward Kingston Wood, the silence was only broken by the noise of Grant's car engine.

He thought about starting a conversation, but, given the woman's state of mind, he fought back the urge: he needed her as calm as possible.

Fear, worry, excitement, trepidation mingled within Grant, forming a vicious cyclone of nausea inside him. He could not remember the last time he'd felt so ill, not even on his first date with Emily when they went rowing on the river. They got to the centre island with a picnic and spent the rest of the day staring at the sky, holding hands, smiling. The beautiful Emily. Emily, who he would propose to that night.

No matter how hard he tried to keep his mind on the job, he could not stop thinking about her. He loved her so much. Emily was so beautiful, so kind, so loving, so caring, so wonderful, so selfless.

Before he knew it, they were at the edge of the wood. Fall colors, with red and orange leaves, brought life to the forest floor. *Gorgeous*, Grant thought to himself. How could something so incredible hold secrets so awful?

Grant's phone vibrated as he closed the car door.

Unsure of what to say to whoever was calling, he decided it would be better to ignore the phone as they left the car to find the body.

Before they had even stepped foot in the wood, the screaming woman careered into the trees like an enraged bison.

Grant picked up speed to catch up with her: he couldn't allow someone else to be hurt. He wouldn't. He could not lose her and, in her frame of mind, she posed a threat to herself and the public.

It wasn't difficult to know where the screaming woman was: he just had to follow her piercing shrieks. As he got closer, the screaming sounded more and more like deranged, excited cackles.

He entered a clearing and suddenly knew something was wrong. Something he could not, and would not, understand before it was too late.

The woman was nowhere to be seen then.

There was no body.

There was nowhere to run if the need arose.

Searching frantically through his pockets for his phone, realisation plunged into him like a bullet: he'd left it in the car.

He was isolated.

Sweat rushed from his face and his heart beat at a deadly pace. What had he gotten himself into?

No, he chastised himself furiously. *Be brave. Do not show fear.*

You're being irrational, he told himself over and over, trying to convince himself of the lie. He had seen how distraught the young woman was, but he had nothing to fear. *Did he?*

Behind him, a twig snapped. Leaves crunched. Still, he was alone.

Grant reached for his gun and terror flowed through his blood: the gun was gone.

Defenceless, vulnerable, alone, Grant's mind blurred. He had to run, get out of these woods, but he couldn't. His legs refused to obey his brain's instructions.

He thought about screaming for help. Was that sensible? Was now the time to be sensible? Or should he just run? What should he do? What was there to do?

Once again, silence ruled. Grant could only hear his rapid heartrate. What was going on? Why was this happening? *What* was happening?

He wanted to scream her name, but did not know it. However, soon enough, a voice was heard.

"I knew I would get you someday," a woman he did not know said happily, casually.

Grant swerved and looked his adversary up and down. In front of him stood not the frightened woman he knew from the town, but an enraged manifestation of hatred, holding a gun, pointing it at his chest.

"It's okay." His voice was soft, as calm as he could make it. "Just give me the gun."

"You *really* are a fool," she spat. "You are not getting out of this."

"Why?" Grant asked, the calmness of his voice gone. "Why are you doing this?"

The screaming woman pointed the gun at the sky and pulled the trigger.

A chillingly proud smile appeared on her face as she lowered the firearm and pointed it at him again. Never had he seen so much loathing in someone's eyes. So much pride. Never would he again.

"Where did that blood come from?" he whispered.

Grant was not really interested in the answer he was just stalling, looking frantically for a way to escape.

The screaming woman giggled, then let out a piercing, squeal of a laugh. "It came from my neighbor." She guffawed as she finished her sentence. "He had it coming."

Her voice emanated joy. Glee. Nausea replaced Grant's desperation.

"Why are you doing this?" he repeated. Again, he did not care.

He wanted to see Emily again.

How was this going to turn out?

"Tell me why you are doing this."

"You ruined me. Took my childhood and destroyed it. For what? Protocol?"

It was the first time he had seen the woman's anger begin to waver, giving way to heartache. Masterfully though, she seemed to then push it back inside. "My parents did their best," she screeched. "You cannot help being born into the situation they were, the situation I was born into. They did what had to be done to ensure I didn't go to bed without food in my stomach. You stormed in and took them away from me. Just like that, they were gone. Because of you, I ended up on the streets. That so-called home you put me in *hated* me." She paused, and cocked her weapon. "A family took me in. True, they looked after me. But, I never forgot the man who stole my family—"

"Listen, I—"

She fired into the sky once again. "Quiet. I have been searching you out for years. Plotting my revenge. Now, I will have it."

"Who are you? I don't know who you think I am—"

"Don't you remember me, Sheriff Carter?" she hissed venomously, before giggling and swaying back and forth, never taking her eyes off him.

"What? I'm not--"

She fired before he could finish the sentence. Two bullets ripped through him.

He fell to the ground as the veins in his chest burst.

He did not die straight away. He lived long enough to see her smirking as she kneeled over him and whispered, "I told you I would kill you for what you did to me, Carter."

The last thing he heard was her glad laughter as she left him in the clearing as food for the animals.

As Grant's life slipped away from him, he thought about the wonderful years he had spent with Emily and all the years they would never get to share. Those decades he had planned. The children they had wanted would never be born. He would never be a father.

Tears of blood streamed from his body. Alone in the clearing, Grant took his final breath.

Her Day Off

This story is dedicated to Marcus who has helped me in so many ways, and who was the first to read this. Thank you, Marcus.

Charlotte's alarm did not wake her up on the twenty-fourth of June. Instead, the gentle glow of sunlight shone serenely through her window, illuminating the room in a gorgeous orange and rousing her from her dreams. She could hear melodious birdsong as she slowly opened her eyes and she smiled. Today was her first day off in months and she was going to enjoy every moment, savor every second.

Leisurely, she kicked the soft covers away. Her heat was on to a pleasurable temperature, rather than roasting her, as it usually did when her husband, Robert, was home. He had an oddly low tolerance of the cold, forever claiming to be freezing … even when it was so unbearably hot that Charlotte thought she was about to expire right there on the living room couch. Since he had to go to work early today, however, Charlotte had set the thermostat to a moderate temperature. *Nice change*, she thought cheerfully to herself as she swayed to sitting.

As she did so, she slipped her feet into her beautifully soft slippers, strolled across the floor to her oak wardrobe, pulled her light-pink silk robe off of its hanger and draped it around herself. Waltzing over to the drapes, she couldn't help but be excited at the prospect of having a stress-free day. There would be no anxiety. She just *knew* that today was going to be blissfully peaceful, with no need to rush around, too busy to live. Oh, yes. She was going to enjoy her day off. After all, she hadn't had one in nearly six months, including weekends.

After opening the drapes, shrouding herself in glorious sunlight, she unlatched the window, pushing it open. The birdsong streamed towards her even louder. Tranquillity. The sun shone warmly and Charlotte embraced its heat with loving arms. Not a cloud spoiled the view. The day was simply perfect.

Turning her head to look at the clock, a small laugh rose up from her very core: nine-fifteen. She had slept in, a luxury she had not enjoyed in … oh, at least a year. Charlotte closed the window and went to get ready. She was in no rush.

***

Next door, Lynette Harrison's day had not got off to as good a start as Charlotte's. Eerie silence reigned over her house. She could only hear her erratic heartbeat, her hurried breathing. Lynette, twenty-years-old, was living alone for the first time in the home of her deceased parents.

Her parents had left her everything – everything including their debts to loan sharks … loan-sharks infamous in Walsington, a small city in South Carolina. Desperate to pay off the mountainous payments, Lynette had had to resort to selling everything. Literally everything. Well, apart from the house. The house, however, was empty, except for essential utilities. In spite of her tireless efforts, the debts remained though. How could she pay them off? Altogether, they amounted to over eight hundred thousand dollars. Plus interest.

Although she couldn't explain why exactly, Lynette had an unshakeable feeling that they – the loan sharks – were coming to collect their money that day. Understanding their several notes fully, she was of the opinion that, when they came, they would be leaving with one of two things: their money … or her life.

Subconsciously, she spent hours staring out her dirty front window, her breath forming a cloud on the glass, temporarily obstructing what little she could see.

I'm going to die. I'm going to die. I'm going to die.

She could feel the aridness of her throat. She should have a drink of water, but that would mean taking her eyes off the driveway. That would mean being unprepared. She was *not* going to do that.

They're coming for me. They're coming for me. They're coming for me.

In a panic, or maybe as a last resort, although Lynette did not – and never had – believed in any deity, she fell to her knees. She was doing what she had promised herself she would never do. She started to pray to any God that would listen.

***

Charlotte, now showered and dressed, danced downstairs, her phone playing the *Nutcracker* score. Ever since she was a child of five when her grandparents had taken her to see the *Swan Lake* ballet, she had adored the glorious music. Completely entranced, its spell still had her under its power twenty-four years later, and now she was an up-and-coming opera singer, having trained in one of the most prestigious houses in the country. Her tutor had told her she could become the next big thing in opera. Nothing Charlotte had even been told had meant so much.

Nothing, that is, apart from when her husband told her he loved her for the very first time. Five-and-a-half years of marriage later, she still woke up every morning in utter disbelief: her husband still loved her.

While eating breakfast, Charlotte opened up her daily planner, picked up a pen, and nearly started writing. *No*, she chastised herself. *Just live a little.* Charlotte had neurotically and meticulously planned every day of her life for the previous few months. She needed a plan to be able to work effectively. *But you're not working today*, she reminded herself, closing the planner.

On top of her opera training, she volunteered in a soup kitchen, making soup for the homeless. On top of that, she worked as an accountant to make a living, her gruelling paperwork increasing by the second. On top of that, she tutored high school students in Mathematics.

She didn't need to work, exactly. Not in reference to a financial need. No, she just wanted to help as many people as she could. Today was literally her first day off in what felt like eons. Today would entail no strenuous workloads, no training, no rushing. Yes, she was going to have a restful day, beginning with a walk around the neighborhood.

So, she ate her cereal leisurely, enjoying the music. When she had finished, she washed the dishes and left, passing the mailman on her way out. In fact, Charlotte just about knocked the man off his feet as they collided. Always one for making an effort to know people who are mostly ignored in her town, Charlotte said, "So sorry, Steven!" She practically sang the words; Charlotte's happiness – her unusually *pure* happiness – was unrestrained, not unlike her kindness. "How are you?"

"I'm great, thank you, Miss Hawthorne. How about you?" Steve answered, searching through the letters in his hand.

"I'm doing well, thank you. Any mail?"

He handed her the letters, smiled, and the pair parted ways.

Assuming there would not be anything of interest or importance, Charlotte tossed the mail onto the couch back inside the house, and left for her walk, blissfully unaware of what she'd just thrown away.

***

Lynette, now beside herself with horrific panic, sat on the floor under her window, curled into a ball, and rocking. Cowering with wide-eyed fear, she silently prayed that anybody who may come would be unable to see her, would think she was out.

You can't hide here, a voice said. The voice of her mother. Realising the accuracy of that statement, yet refusing to rise above the windowsill, Lynette slid across the floor, heading for the front door. A rattling of metal sent Lynette scuttling backwards.

The mailman. She didn't have to open the envelopes to know they were all bills.

After waiting for several minutes, she defiantly decided she was not going to die. Not there. Not now.

She didn't put on a jacket, but leaped to her feet. Lynette flung her door open just as a black car with tinted windows pulled up at the foot of her drive.

***

Practically skipping around the local park, Charlotte couldn't help but appreciate the world around her – appreciate it like she never had before. The flowers, bright as a midsummer's day. The grass, greener than the ripest apple. The sky, bluer than ever before. All of the people there with their children sent a surge of energy through Charlotte. She only had eight hours to wait before she could tell her husband the news – the news they had been waiting for since they married. That, she decided, was what she was going to spend her day doing: seeing where, in a matter of months, they could take their child, their beautiful little girl.

Everything had been planned out. Charlotte and Robert had had, at the very least, twenty conversations on the subject of how they would raise their child if they were ever blessed enough to have one.

She would be called Arial because it means strength. She would be raised in a loving home, with a devoted mother and father. As soon as she was born, Charlotte planned to stop working so she could focus on being the mother Arial deserved.

Although they had the money to buy several vacation homes, and had long debated purchasing one in the South of France, they'd decided against it: they wanted their daughter to have one home.

A home is a place of love, of safety, of unity, not brokenness. Charlotte's parents divorced when she was three-years-old, and, for months, she had been practically ignored by both parties. Until, that is, they fought over who got custody. Her mother won. Being split between two homes completely removed all meaning and sentiment, leaving both abodes as nothing but bricks and mortar. They meant nothing to Charlotte. She didn't grow up in a home, but houses. Therefore, it was concluded that their daughter was going to grow up in one home as the centre of attention.

Listening to birdsong as she strolled through the park, Charlotte hummed soothing lullabies to herself – the ones she would sing to Arial.

Having reached the park exit, Charlotte headed home, basking in the warm sunlight.

***

In front of Lynette stood three heavily- built men, all of them paler than the dead. There was a clear leader: the man walking straight toward her, a ravenous grin plastered across his face. Lynette could tell he wanted her to run. Like a lion, these men would enjoy the hunt. His eyes, blacker than space, were unforgiving, uncaring, vacant.

Lynette could feel her legs shaking, her knees threatening to buckle. Yet she refused to betray the fear circulating her body. She stood her ground.

Run, fool, a voice told her. *You could run and find a neighbor. Get help.*

She valiantly fought the urge. She wasn't going to bring another innocent person into this, the way her parents had brought her into it.

Scream, the voice echoed in her mind. *Scream. Run. Do something.*

As if he had read her mind, the leader hissed, "Don't do anything stupid, Lynny."

Her heart was going at a speed of knots. Still, she stood firm. If she could help it, she wouldn't give him *any* satisfaction of knowing how terrified she was or how uncaring she was about dying ... how ready she was.

No, she chastised herself, defiance suddenly pumping through her. *You are* not *going to die. You're going to get through this. You are going to survive.*

"You owe me money," he snarled, rolling his tongue inside his cheek as he finished the sentence. *Me*, he said. Not *us*. He was going to enjoy this, Lynette knew. She knew he was going to take his time to make her suffer as much as he could. "We are here to collect it."

He grabbed her by the wrist and tossed her into the house so hard she was thrown off her feet. Lynette hit her head on the foot of the stairs and cried out as pain rushed viciously through her.

Before Lynette could raise a hand to nurse the injury, the leader had pounced. He grabbed her by the hair, effortlessly picked her up, and threw her back down. Lynette could do nothing to stop the beating, nothing to stop the door being shut, and nothing to stop the drapes being drawn. She was defenceless.

But she was going to endure it all. She would not show fear.

***

Charlotte strolled down the street and into her perfectly warm home, where the mail was waiting. Rather than opening it straightaway, Charlotte went to make herself a cup of coffee.

It the machine gurgled, she hummed beautiful lullabies to herself. As she did so, she pulled open a drawer, and took out the sonogram image.

Her doctors had tried in vain to persuade Charlotte to tell her husband about their baby before the sonogram. She would have, but she didn't want to tell him in case something went wrong.

Joyous tears flowed out of her eyes as she gazed at the black-and-white image of their beautiful daughter – of Arial.

Still holding the sonogram, she poured water into the mug, and walked over to read the mail. Smiling out at her incredibly safe suburban street, she thought about how adorable it would be to see Arial running around in the following years. *Oh yes,* thought Charlotte to herself, *Arial will be safe here.*

While doing so, she happened to glance out the window, spotting a liquorice-black car. Although she thought it was odd that she hadn't seen the car before, she assumed it must belong to Lynette. This thought pleased her: Lynette was treating herself. She'd had such a rough time of late, so she deserved it.

She placed her coffee down on the center unit, and opened the mail. The first letter was from her cousin in Australia, filling her in on all the news of her life. The second letter was stuck to the envelope underneath. Scrawled in a what could only be a child's penmanship were the words: *Have the money ready by ten o'clock on Monday. Or you know what will happen.*

Charlotte flipped the envelope over, and it had Lynette's address on it. Like a wall collapsing onto her, Charlotte realised the black car wasn't Lynette's. Eyes widened, heart pounding, Charlotte looked to the clock. Ten-thirty-one. Lynette was in very real danger.

Charlotte didn't know how she knew, and she didn't care how she knew. Snatching her phone out of her pocket, she dialed 911.

"Hello, what is your emergency?" the operator said, her voice cold, unconcerned.

"My neighbor is in danger." Charlotte said, rattled. "Send help!" She gave the address. "Please send he –"

BOOM.

"Ma'am?" the operator started, her voice panicked. "Ma'am!"

Charlotte was out of the house before the phone hit the ground. The sonogram fell onto the floor.

She banged on Lynette's door, screaming her name, before her own door closed behind her.

***

Stalking around the room, circling Lynette like a vulture, the leader put the gun back into his belt. "You know I am not above killing, little girl. Last chance. Get the money, or I *will* kill you."

"I don't have any money," Lynette wept, all facade of dauntlessness eradicated by the gunshot hole in her kitchen window. She wanted to run, but wouldn't dare. She wanted to scream, but couldn't.

BANG. BANG. BANG. In quick succession, blows rained down on the door. The leader smiled, his teeth showing fully as he licked his lips. He stalked to the window. His hand curled around the drape, pulling it back, his eyes lit up, an explosion of vicious excitement. "Here's lunch," he hissed, his tongue rolling over his teeth.

Sliding over to the door, he concealed his gun in his belt. He wrapped his fingers around the handle, laughing at the desperate, thunderous knocking.

Throwing the door open, he smirked. "Hello, dear," the leader said, bearing his teeth.

Charlotte burst into the house, scanning for Lynette. "The police are on their way," she said to the leader, almost threatening him. Her fearlessness was not feigned. Her determination was not false. Her bravery was absolute. "Oh, sweetie," she cried, falling to her knees to help Lynette up. Lynette tried to speak, but only an incoherent string of noises came out. "Don't worry," she said, completely calm. "We're going to get out of here."

Guffawing, the leader pushed the door shut. Whipping out his gun, he looked Charlotte up and down. "You are just a full-course meal. Shame."

Studiously ignoring him, Charlotte helped Lynette to her feet. Their endeavor was carried out in vain for Lynette fell back to the ground. Charlotte couldn't – no, wouldn't – think of anything other than getting her to safety. She simply would not let herself think of the alternative. No. There was no alternative. "Come on, Lynette!" she whispered. "We are getting out of here. The police are coming."

Again, the leader laughed. This time, however, his laugh hinted at the nervous tension that was rushing through him. He was running out of time. He had to get this over with. "See," he said, "I know you are pretty. But, at least try not to be so abnormally stupid."

Continuing to block him out, Charlotte half-walked-half-carried Lynette over to the door. "It's entertaining that you believe either of you are going to walk out of here. You're not leaving without a body bag."

"The police are on their way," Charlotte snapped back again, her voice surprisingly calm and collected. No fear was shown. No fear was felt. But then ... but then ...

She remembered her baby. The unborn child resting trustingly within her. She *had* to get out of there. Fast. And she was going to. She was going to get out of there with Lynette. Lynette was going to survive. Charlotte was going to survive. And her baby ... her baby was going to survive.

"We'll be long gone before they get here." With a sadistic flick of the hand, the leader locked the door. As if by telepathic demand, the henchmen seized Charlotte and Lynette. They forced them onto their knees, holding the pair still with ease.

"The police are coming," Charlotte whispered to Lynette, her statement confirmed by the sounding of far-off sirens. A sigh of relief.

"I'll make short work of this," the leader snapped, suddenly anxious. He pointed the gun at Lynette. He pulled the trigger. Lynette Harrison fell to the ground.

"I'm pregnant," Charlotte wept, ashamed of her panic before she'd even finished her sentence.

"That's not going to save you."

"Our Father who art in Heaven, hallowed be thy name, thy –"

Charlotte never finished the prayer.

***

Robert was in a meeting when his assistant, Louisa, received the call. The cacophonous ringing commenced at one-minute-after-twelve.

"Hello, Robert Hawthorne's office, Louisa speaking, how can I help?" the assistant droned, having said this at least two thousand times that year.

"Is Mr Hawthorne available?" Mrs MacMillan, the receptionist, asked, her voice strangled.

"No. He's in a meeting."

"You need to get him out. Now. Two police officers are here. They need to speak with him immediately."

"Why?" she asked.

"Something about his wife, but they won't tell me."

"Where are they?"

"In the reception."

"I'll get him." Louisa hung up the phone, and sprinted across the floor. Bursting into the conference room, all eyes turned to her. "Mr Hawthorne, I'm sorry to interrupt. You have people who need to see you."

Irate, as he usually was when he had to talk to his team, he snapped, "Louisa, I am in a meeting!"

"It's urgent," Louisa barked back. "Two police officers. It's about your wife."

Like a bull, Robert was out of the room, speeding through the building, colliding with just about everything in his path. He cascaded into the elevator, where the radio was blaring. "*News just in. There has been a shooting in a suburban street. Two are confirmed dead.*"

He bolted into the foyer. "She's not, is she?" was all he could manage. Both officers, clearly new to the job, looked at each other, both waiting for the other to pass on the news. Their silence spoke volumes. "What's happened to Charlotte?" he boomed, his words anguished, his throat dry.

The officer on the left stepped forward. "I'm very sorry to tell you that your wife has been in an accident. She lost a lot of blood and—"

Robert hit the floor in an explosion of hysterical screams. "Not true."

All Robert could do was shake, scream. He didn't try to stay calm. He didn't try to do anything. He only thought of Charlotte.

That morning he hadn't kissed her goodbye: he had been too busy, too unwilling to wake her. Now, he would never kiss her again, never see her smile again, never hear her laugh. Charlotte. Charlotte.

Her name, as beautiful as she. *Too busy*, he remembered. *Too busy to kiss my wife goodbye.*

Robert hadn't wanted to be late for work. He put himself before Charlotte. Now she was gone. He would never forgive himself.

Charlotte's face, her beautiful face, flashed into his vision before – before everything crashed in around him … before he lost consciousness.

***

A week later, Charlotte and Lynette's faces were splashed across the national papers. There was not a person in the state who didn't know their names.

It was the day before Charlotte's funeral was due to take place. Robert was driving home for the first time since his darling wife had been killed. Nothing about the street, the street he and Charlotte had picked out together because of its 'cosiness', looked familiar. Nothing. He may as well have driven to a state he'd never been to.

Lynette's house had been surrounded by flowers, as had the house he lived in with Charlotte. Hundreds upon hundreds of them.

When will this nightmare end?

He had spent the last week going over things in his mind. *How could this have happened? Why? Who would want to hurt Charlotte?*

All she ever did was her best for everybody else. Charlotte would never hurt anybody. In fact, Robert was convinced she was incapable of it. Why would anyone hurt her?

The police presence was still heavy. Not that he cared. He didn't care much if the world ended that night. He wasn't living. He was surviving. They are two different things. All he wanted was to be with Charlotte. All he longed for was to see her face. All he desired was her safety. He had promised to protect her. He had broken his promise.

Robert walked up his path, ready for a confrontation with the police officer standing at the door.

"Really?" the officer snapped. "You lot are vultures, thinking you can come here for dirt on the family and —"

"What are you talking about?" Robert muttered angrily. "I live here."

After consulting his superior, the officer agreed to let Robert in. "Apologies, sir."

Without answering, he walked into the house. Immediately, the gorgeous aroma of Charlotte hit Robert, mingling with the smell of coffee. Sure enough, there it was on the table … Charlotte's last cup of coffee, the cup she didn't get to finish.

Refusing to allow tears to form, Robert drifted upstairs into the walk-in closet. Not wanting to stay any longer than was absolutely necessary, he scanned the closet for the suit Charlotte liked most on him. It was located easily: having had an *interesting* sense of humour, Charlotte had organised all the clothes in Robert's closet based on how much she liked them.

The memory of her expressions when she saw his beach shirts brought a painful smile to his face. It was the first time he had smiled in a week, and it lasted less than a second: he remembered instantly he would never see that expression again … he would never see Charlotte again. He would never hug her again.

He took the suit, and headed downstairs. Again, that cup of coffee caught his eye. But, there was something else beside it. Thanks to the sun, he saw a coat of dust obscuring an image. From his standpoint, it looked like a photograph.

He placed his suit down on the sofa, and picked up the picture. Not particularly caring, he wiped the dust off with his sleeve. A sonogram. Written on the back was the nineteenth of February and, in Charlotte's handwriting: "We're gonna be parents, Rob!"

Relentless, acidic pain burst out of his heart and pumped through him, eroding him from the inside. No words could do justice to the nothingness he was experiencing. It was as if his life was being sucked out of him – what was left of it, at any rate.

Robert tried to cry. Tried so hard. But no tears came. His suffering was too profound to be released. Fire roared within him. His throat, arid and scorched, stung as he tried to swallow. Tried to breathe. *I will kill whoever did this. I will find them and make them suffer.*

Although he knew he wasn't thinking straight, he couldn't help but notice the appeal of his thoughts. Killing them wouldn't bring his family back to him. Killing them wouldn't stop the suffering. Killing them wouldn't help. No, there was only one thing that would help: seeing Charlotte again. Robert knew that was impossible without harming himself, without ending his life. That was another alluring thought – however, he knew Charlotte would never forgive him if he harmed himself to be with her.

But he could. Even if she hated him for it, he would be with her …

His train of thought was derailed when a police officer walked in, his face void of emotion. "Nice place," he mumbled.

Robert pocketed the sonogram, vowing to carry his baby with him wherever he went. He was a father now and nobody could take that away from him.

They could take the future he had planned with Charlotte, the future with their child. They could take their child's graduations and wedding, the special moments they would have seen and cherished. They could take the family adventures they would have enjoyed. They could take it all. And they had. Never, though, could they take the bond that made the three of them a family. Nothing could sever their love.

He forced himself up onto his feet and headed for the door.

***

Sitting at the front of the church, listening to the weeping of the organ, Robert realised just how wrong it was. Charlotte was a fun, loving, bubbly person, with a real zest for life. He knew, if she were looking down now, seeing all this hurt, she would be heartbroken. Although he couldn't stop that corrosive pain, he wished he could. For her.

Robert didn't speak to anyone as they filed into the room. Nor did he notice when the music stopped.

No. He was away with Charlotte, back on their vacation to Europe seven years ago. They went to Dubrovnik in Croatia. For the two of them, it was the first time leaving the States. They adored that trip. He proposed there. He remembered the color of the sky as vividly as he remembered Charlotte: an explosion of beauty, brilliant oranges mixing with reds. He half-smiled as he thought of it.

A gentle nudge from his mother ripped him from his memory, and told him it was time to go onto the platform.

Again, forcing every movement, he walked to the microphone. "Five-and-a-half years we were married," he began, already struggling to keep himself composed. *You promised yourself you wouldn't do this*, he chastised himself. "Eight years as a couple. Ten years we knew each other. I remember the first day we met. I was convinced I was hallucinating: that would be the only explanation for her unearthly beauty. I was amazed, stunned.

"Her beauty," he continued, "was not what made her so attractive though: it was her attitude. She lit up every room simply by being in it. She brought a smile to everyone's face – everyone, including those she didn't know. Charlotte never walked by anyone without smiling at them, without talking to them, without making them feel special, loved. Almost always, she would get a smile back. Always, actually. My darling Charlotte was just the kind of person who was loved by everybody who knew her. She lit up my life, and if you look outside now, you will see she is lighting up the sky. Leading me forward. She is the stars of the night, the sun of the day. She is the morning's birdsong."

With every word he said, Robert's composure declined. He stood silently for several seconds, looking at the casket which contained his wife, trying to decide whether or not to let everyone know about her pregnancy. After a pause, he pulled the sonogram out of his pocket. "According to the police officers, Charlotte heard the first gunshot and, with absolutely no thoughts of her own safety, ran toward it. To help. You see, everything Charlotte did was for other people. She passed away the way she lived: selflessly helping others."

After kissing the sonogram, he finished with, "Charlotte, my dear, precious, darling Charlotte, my heart is broken and will not heal until I hold you in my arms once more. But, for now, my love, take our baby. You have earned your wings, too soon, my darling. Fly away to the land where there are no tears and no suffering. No hurt. I love you. Forever and always."

Outside, in the glorious sunlight, Charlotte was laid to rest.

***

That afternoon, Lynette's funeral took place. She didn't have any family left alive, so, Charlotte's family attended. There was no ceremony, just a burial.

Robert gave her eulogy. "Lynette Harrison lived here for twenty years. Her parents took their own lives several months ago. I can't say I knew them well. I can't say I made an effort to, which I will regret for the rest of my days. Charlotte knew Lynette well enough to speak to. I never made the effort. Nevertheless, I owe Lynette everything. Thanks to her, my darling didn't die alone. The last thing they saw was the face of a friend. For that, I am eternally grateful." Pausing to keep himself composed, he exhaled a breath he didn't know he had been holding. "Lynette has been portrayed as the cause of the murders. No fault lies with victims. Lynette, I am sorry I didn't know you. I hope you have the peace you deserve."

Turning to face the people, he continued, "We must not allow anger to fester in us. We must not seek revenge. Our revenge will be taking our lives back. We will not be beaten, we will not cower from hate. No, we will dwell in love."

In the warm of the afternoon sun, Lynette was buried.

Andrew Lamont

When Things Go Wrong

Dedicated to Ben Morley, who believed in this story before I did. Thank you, Ben.

It wasn't supposed to happen this way. Nobody was supposed to die. How could things have gone so disastrously wrong? Actions speak louder than words. It's a well-known phrase that's been drummed into me since I was an innocent little child. But I'm not little anymore. I'm not innocent anymore. I'm a murderer.

It started the day my little brother, Jack, burst through the door, weeping and bleeding. I assumed he had fallen so, as he galloped upstairs, I walked to the cupboard under the stairs, picked up the first-aid kit and headed quietly up the stairs.

Normally, when someone was in the state my brother was in, I'd be expected by most to run after him. What most fail to realise is that Jack has Autistic Spectrum Disorder. He always has and he always will. His hatred of his uniqueness is devastating. I've spent years trying to impress upon him the benefits of autism. To no avail. Jack is one of the stubbornest people I know and he doesn't seem to understand or believe that nobody has ever changed the world by blending in. I always ask him why he would want to be just someone else in the crowd who nobody notices. Why he would want to be rid of the very thing that makes him stand out, the part of him that makes him who he is? Why would he want to change himself to fit with societal normalities?

What is more, Jack is one of those incredibly lucky people – whether he realises it or not – with more than one 'stand-out attribute'. By that I mean, he has autism, Attention Deficit Hyperactivity Disorder and Sensory Integration Disorder. Perhaps I'm being deeply unhelpful and unrealistically optimistic but, for Jack's sake as well as my own, I *have* to believe in silver linings. There's a positive to be found in almost all situations, if you look hard enough. For me at least, the harder I look to discover a positive, the more I appreciate it.

Due to Jack's so-called disorders – in particular, his SID – he despises sudden loud noises, especially if they sound like they're coming towards him. My brother is slightly unpredictable with noises, however: if he knows one is coming, sometimes he'll be *okay* with it – other times, he'll have a full-blown meltdown. It's terrible to witness, especially when you know there is nothing you can do to help. So, while still moving as quickly as I could, I ascended with what I like to think was an elegant silence.

Standing outside his door, I could hear his favourite song: *Be Alright* by Ariana Grande. I listened out for its beat: ever since that day in the hospital, Jack has played the song whenever melancholy sets in. Reaching my hand out, I knocked on the door twice in speedy succession – a routine I employ as it makes Jack feel safe … I don't know why. I don't need to know why because if it makes Jack feel safe, I'll do it.

Slowly, Jack opened the door. Upon seeing him closely, it was obvious he had not fallen simply due to lack of awareness of his surroundings. There may be a medical diagnosis to explain Jack's societally-labelled "clumsiness", but he has received no such diagnosis. Red tears streamed down his face. His right eye was swollen and beginning to purple. His lip was split, but had stopped bleeding. Someone had attacked him.

"Can I come in, please?" I asked, striving to keep my voice from betraying the mixture of anger and despair rising within me. I received a nod in response, but no words. With Jack, you always know he is deeply unhappy when he doesn't speak. More often than not, it's impossible to get him to be quiet.

Another huge giveaway was that Jack was wearing his crown: he only ever wore it when he needed to feel strong and powerful. And safe.

Jack's main obsession was historical monarchs. He believed his crown protected him, so it did. Whenever he wears it, bravery flows through him.

Not that, without it, he's cowardly. He is brave; he just doesn't know it.

Studiously attempting to appear calm, I walked towards his desk. As it turned out, I executed my endeavour poorly: Jack asked me why I was trying so hard to hide something. Despite everything, I smiled. I should've remembered it is futile to try to keep something from Jack: he notices everything.

I sat down on his desk chair, trying not to look at the desk which was covered with printed pictures of kings and queens. Jack, still wearing his crown, sat opposite me. While I was nursing his injuries, Jack recited the Declaration of Arbroath. He learned it five years before – at the age of seven.

Be Alright finished and restarted, as Jack proudly expounded the ancient words. He grimaced, squinted and pulled away when I cleaned the cut on his lip.

Once I'd attended to his injuries – and once he had finished his dramatic rendition of the Declaration – I asked him, "Who did this to you?"

Jack, by means of reply, stood up, power-walked to his cupboard, went in and sat down and closed the door.

"Avoid the question all you want," I said. "It won't stop me asking. "

I could almost feel Jack's eye-roll. His sigh was audible – almost amusingly so. The door clicked open and Jack emerged from the shadows. "He didn't know what he was doing," he whimpered. "He doesn't understand."

My brother's compassion left me in a state of eternal awe. In spite of all his – for lack of a better word – issues, he cares *so* deeply for other people. All he wants to do is help others. I remember one Christmas morning, Jack was clearly upset. I didn't understand why … at all. So, I asked. "I'm thinking of all the people who have no presents to wake up to," he told me.

The fact that people have it in their heart to discriminate is a poison dagger to my heart. Before being told, it was obvious that whoever did this to

Jack did it because he is different, because they do not understand him – because they don't *want* to understand him. Although Jack, to the point of absurdity, tries to see the best in everyone, I think some people are just cruel for the sake of it. For the sake of it. I don't even think it's because of their supposed insecurities: some people are horrible and enjoy being unreasonable. And, before I'd even been told who did it, I had suspicions.

"It was …" He swallowed – well, it was more of a fearful gulp – and then he forced the words out: "Damien Sinclair."

Bile made its way into my mouth from my pure, unadulterated anger. Damien Sinclair is one of those people who are just plain vile: he has no redeeming qualities whatsoever and no remorse for the pain he inflicts on those he considers to be inferior. He is an emotional parasite sucking the happiness out of society.

Perhaps that sounds harsh; so, I'll put everything into context: for as long as I have known him, Damien has victimised anybody he views as weak, or different. There is a lengthy list of targets. I used to be one of them. He stopped when I fought back. It's usually the same with bullies: they pride themselves on looking tough when targeting those who are incapable – or unwilling – to defend themselves.

Although I didn't feel a specific need to enquire about Damien's motives, I asked if Jack had *any* idea why Damien attacked him.

Immediately after asking, I wish I had not: Jack's legs went out from under him, bringing him crashing to the ground.

"Why am I hated?" he sobbed, his words conjoining so they neared incoherence. He removed his crown and whispered, "Why can't everything just stop? What is the point in everything? Hatred is taking over. Wherever you look, there it is. Why can't everyone just get along?"

Jack looked at his crown, lying on the floor and put it into his cupboard.

"Look, it is true to say that this world has hatred in it. But it is also true to say love and light will drown out the darkness of hatred."

He replied, "All the world needs is a little love. Why am I such a freak?"

Rushing to his side, I wrapped him in my arms. "You're not a freak," I told him. "You're unique and —"

"Then why do so many people hate me?" He didn't just sob through his words ... he quietly wailed them.

Words can be small, they can be large. But they are mighty. They can build people up until who they were is less than half of who they've become. Just as easily, however, they can destroy someone.

Shakespeare wrote, "The pen is mightier than the sword." He was correct and it is a truth that has lasted to this day and will endure the test of time. But without action, words are meaningless. Actions speak louder.

"They don't *hate* you," I said, trying and failing to be consoling. I've never been a comforting person because nobody has ever comforted me. Not properly. So, I just don't know how to do it. "They definitely don't hate you. They just don't understand you and they're threatened by you. That can be changed."

"How?" he asked me. Before I could answer, my brother's pain deepened. "I don't want to upset anybody." With every word, Jack's crying intensified. I cannot over-emphasise how caring he is: no matter how much he is put through, he will adore others. "I want everyone to be friends. Friendships makes us stronger. You can't survive in this world alone. It just doesn't work like that. *Everybody* deserves friends."

He wrapped his arms around me and there we sat for thirty minutes – or thereabouts. There are no bonds like those with a loving family.

After that half hour had passed, Jack raised his head, so his eyes briefly met mine, before soaring to look at something above my head. I knew what he wanted. Anybody who knew my brother knew of his deep love for football.

We jumped to our feet, Jack got the ball and we headed outside into the mild heat. Though they be far and few between, Scottish summers can be warm. Happily, this was one of them. I love Scotland, don't get me wrong. It is no secret that I am glad we moved here. The *only* negative is the dramatic dip anybody would experience after moving across the Atlantic from Texas – and, boy, was it dramatic.

Jack and I kicked the ball around for a while before going back inside. Although there can be half-summery weather in Scotland, there'll likely never be one without rain. The clouds rolled in quicker than I'd expected.

I can't remember much of Texas, to be honest: I was only five when we moved. All my memories are of summer, which probably explains why I noticed the heat difference.

"I don't understand," Jack said, his eyes threatening to tear up again, "why people bully. What do they stand to achieve?" He wasn't upset for himself, I knew that: he was saddened by the pain others experience.

"I can't give you an answer, Jack," I replied. "I wish I could. I guess it's because they are hurting themselves." I didn't believe my words. Some people bully for the simple reason that they can. They get a thrill from inflicting pain. It's disgusting, but true.

"I wish it would stop. I wish I wasn't hated."

Venom surged through me, eroding my heart, until all I could feel was burning. Catching myself in the mirror, seeing my aggressively reddened face, I noticed my fists were clenched; I was shaking. *Don't*, I warned myself. *Don't lose control.*

"You're not hated," I told him, through gritted teeth. "I *promise*," I snarled, "I will make the bullying stop."

Jack smiled meekly, striving to conceal his pain, which only intensified my anger. "How?" he asked.

"I don't know yet, but I will."

***

My alarm went off like a siren at six o'clock the following morning. Although I was already awake, I didn't want it to sound: sometimes when you're lying in bed is the best time to think.

As I got myself ready for school, all I could think about was how I could help Jack. I would keep him with me during breaks. No, that wouldn't help. What would he do once I left school? I could go to the Head … No, that would make things worse.

Knowing my best friend, Charlie, would be awake, I phoned him and explained the situation and asked his advice. Even though I'm older than him, I see him as an older brother. I'm forever going to him for guidance and he always gives me what I need. It's not always what I want to hear, but I can be guaranteed that what he's saying will help. After telling him about Jack and Damien, I asked, "What do I do? How do I get this sorted without making things worse for Jack?"

Rather like with Jack, I could sense Charlie rolling his eyes at me. "I have one question," he said. "Are you looking for revenge or resolution?"

"Both."

"Getting revenge is never the answer: revenge breeds anger, bitterness and more hatred. Your desire for revenge will never be satisfied; you'll live your life believing they deserved worse."

"How can I stop this?" I asked, desperately longing for a straightforward answer.

"You are not going to like what I have to say," Charlie told me.

"Aren't you the one who told me that help isn't always easy to receive?"

"You need to talk to Damien," he began. His words were followed by a pause. After several seconds, he continued, "It's obvious he's threatened in some way by Jack. He doesn't understand your brother, and needs to be educated. Understanding others isn't a quick process, but it is a worthwhile one: when you can empathise, or even sympathise, with someone who has done you wrong, you see the world clearer. I have to go and do my papers now. Bye! See you at school."

"Bye."

Speak to Damien? Did he actually *suggest* speaking *to him? What was I supposed to say to that animal?*

Jack's alarm blared. He bounded out of his room and down the stairs. The bathroom door slammed.

Speak to Damien, Charlie had said. But what was there to say? How did I know he'd listen? "How do you know he won't?" a voice whispered.

I had nothing to lose and a lot to gain from giving him a chance to change. It sounds clichéd, but I thought it could be true: everybody deserves a second chance. I belong to a minority of the population which believes in giving people two chances. Only. Blow the first one and the trust is gone. Blow the second chance and you're gone.

Charlie's words replayed in my mind: *Understanding others isn't a quick process, but it is a worthwhile one.* Had I ever tried to find out *why*

Damien was like this? There must be a reason. *Maybe he's hurting himself,* an inner voice whispered.

"Or, maybe he's simply nasty," I whispered back. Saying those words – the words I'd lived by for years – suddenly sounded alien to me. When did I become so stubborn?

Going against all of my screaming instincts, I decided to talk to Damien. Nobody has given him the chance to change … maybe that's all he needs.

***

Twenty minutes later, we were sat at the kitchen table eating breakfast. Jack devoured his food in silence. Despite his obvious wish not to talk, I asked, "What classes do you have today?"

He didn't look up, or answer at first. When I asked again though, he replied: "History, then English."

"You only have two lessons?" I jested. "Easy day." Although he tried to fight it, he smiled.

"Maths, Geography and Gym after lunch."

"Did you finish your homework?" I asked. He answered by sprinting through to the living room, crashing around for a couple of minutes, before charging back into the kitchen, cradling several pieces of paper under his arm.

While handing them to me, he told me the subject. After reading through the papers, I handed them back. "Good job, buddy. Go and put them in your bag and get your shoes on. We leave in ten minutes."

After giving me a thumbs-up, he did so. "Is Dad at work again?" he shouted through.

"Yes! He left before we got up."

***

At half-seven, Jack and I left for school. We walked most of the way talking about Henry VIII. I was studying the Tudors in History and continually forgot the order of his wives.

Jack never grew impatient. There wasn't even a flicker of irritation in his voice when he told me – for the hundredth time – that Catherine of Aragon married him first, followed by Anne Boleyn, followed by Jane Seymour, and so on.

His memory astonishes me even to this day. He could remember everything he'd read, and heard, about kings and queens from countless countries.

Everything. I can barely remember how many wives Henry VIII had.

"What happened to them?" I asked, not in the least embarrassed by my distinct lack of intelligence. Jack had the skill of keeping people's self-esteem up, regardless of how pitiful their brain was ... and Jack valued brains.

"Keep it in your mind with a rhyme," he said. "Divorced, beheaded, died. Divorced, beheaded, survived. If it helps," he continued, "put it to a song."

As we turned the corner into the lane that ended across the street from the playground, Charlie sprinted over to us.

"Hey, guys!" he chirped. I'm really not a morning person and his enthusiasm was sickening. I told him this. Every day. It didn't make a difference. Which, I suppose, is a good thing. It's what I say to Jack: don't change yourself to suit others. "How are you, Jack?"

Jack, although he knew Charlie and liked him, didn't tend to speak much when he was around. His shyness is the main reason he doesn't make many friends: he's anxious about saying something stupid in front of someone and losing them. He had a friend for years in primary school, but that "friend" left Jack alone when he found out he was autistic.

I'd like to make it perfectly clear that I don't blame anyone, but the boy's parents. I heard them talking in the playground when I picked Jack up. "You mustn't go near that boy," they had said. "He's got a disease."

I was so shocked that I couldn't say anything. I still can't quite comprehend how somebody can be so ignorant. I pity them honestly. Not in the same way they pity us though. They pity us because we're different. I pity them because they're unwilling to change. I think that philosophy is what convinced me to give Damien a chance.

Instead of speaking, Jack gave Charlie a thumbs-up and smiled.

"Good," Charlie said, even though he knew it was a lie. He asked me how I was doing, and in that very British way, I told him I was fine. He also knew that wasn't true.

When we arrived at school, Charlie and I walked Jack to his registration class, waited for him to go in and for the teacher to arrive.

As soon as Jack had sat down, I practically sprinted to find Damien. Everybody who knew who he was, knew where he hung out before, after, and sometimes during school: behind the bike shelters where he would smoke marijuana or worse.

He would more than likely be surrounded by his cronies – the same ones who used to persecute me because I am a slower learner than Damien is – but I didn't care. I wasn't going to start a fight, or try to intimidate anybody. I just wanted to talk.

Damien, being honest, is indescribably intelligent: he can learn complex mathematical formulae and remember irregular French verbs much quicker than anyone else. I hoped, therefore, that he would listen to what I had to say. Obviously, I was doubtful, but, despite my instincts, I needed to give him a chance. I silently begged for him to have some glimmer of compassion – however small the glimmer was, it would help. Intelligence, without compassion, is meaningless.

The horrendous odour of his marijuana penetrated my nostrils. Bile rose into my mouth. I thought I was going to be sick. I don't know why the smell arouses such a strong reaction within me …

Doing my very best to ignore it, I walked up to Damien. My childhood bully. The nightmares I endured for years because of him filled my mind. I remembered them all so clearly.

My heart raced and my throat dried. *Be brave,* I told myself. I said those words thousands of times through my years of turmoil. Every time I went to school, those words would replay in my mind. Every time I was alone in a corridor, those words would emerge. I hadn't felt the need in months to say them. I guess you never quite forget what it's like to be bullied and it's worse when you come face-to-face with your tormentor. But you just need to live with it.

"Oh, look!" Damien mumbled. "It's little ... Have you come for a beating like the one I gave your retarded brother yesterday?"

His henchmen laughed. A dull cacophony of snorts.

Fire burned through me. My fists clenched of their own volition. My blood scorched my bones. All I could think of doing was taking Damien by the scruff of his neck – as I had done just a few months before – and smashing his head on the corner of a wall.

"Stay calm," Charlie said just loud enough for me to hear him. "He wants a reaction out of you, so that he has an excuse to attack you."

His words hit the nail on the head. Damien was doing this deliberately. Of course he was! He hadn't forgiven me for what I did to him that day. It wasn't in front of anyone. That didn't matter. Damien had waited all these months to get his revenge. Like I said, he was smart. Damien knew he wouldn't be able to beat me if I fought back. That is why he targeted Jack: he knew Jack would not defend himself. Against Damien, he couldn't. In fact, against most, he couldn't. Not through weakness, but through kindness: Jack would rather allow himself to be hurt than inflict pain on someone else.

Before I had even decided to speak, I shouted, "Try it, Sinclair. Go on. Try it. Let's show your little buddies what happens when we have a fair fight."

His face reddened. "I don't know what you're talking about," he snarled. "Mighty big words. Can you back them up with action?"

I nodded as casually as I could. "Want to see me back them up?" I said, hoping Damien would pick up on the threat. He did. Clearly, his memory had brought some sort of sobriety, despite the dope smoke.

"And get myself excluded for beating you to an inch of your life? I think not. What do you want, rodent?"

Now was my chance. Heart racing, throat drying more with every passing second, I said, "I have a few questions for you." Damien raised his eyebrows. "Why do you always go for those who can't defend themselves? Why would you go after my special needs brother, who you *know* is incapable of defending himself because he refuses to fight? Why are you so threatened by things you don't understand?"

"I understand everything I need to," he spat. "I understand your brother, and all those like him, are inferior and deserve everything they get. Society would be so much better without them."

"See," I replied. "That's where you're wrong. Diversity is what makes a society grow. Acceptance is what makes people grow. You," I said and I could feel myself getting more and more enraged with every word I said, getting closer and closer to hitting him, "are what is wrong with society. Narrow-mindedness, cowardice, prejudice. They are traits that need to be purged."

Damien was on his feet in a second, all memory of that former defeat apparently gone. His anger flooded out of him in a tirade of disgusting curses that no respectful human being would ever say. "Calling me a coward?" he concluded.

Knowing exactly what was coming next, I nodded. I didn't care if he tried to attack me. In fact, I wanted him to because then I could do what I did all those months ago. This time, however, I wouldn't try to stop myself. This time there would be witnesses.

"Not on school grounds," he said, smiling. "They can't do anything if this happens off-campus."

We walked out of the school gates. Before I had the chance to do anything, he grabbed me and we were fighting. "Do nothing!" he shouted, as his little bodyguards leapt to their feet, ready to get involved. "I'm going to enjoy this."

We swung each other about, neither of us relenting. I landed a punch and he faltered, dropped his guard. I went ballistic. Punches rained down on him. In one swift movement, he took me off my feet and we were rolling on the grass, landing punches as often as we could, as hard as we could.

I fell away and we jumped to our feet. We ran for each other. I swung him around and let go. He went flying into the road, into the path of a speeding car that nobody had heard. The car thundered into him. Everything went into slow motion. He was thrown onto the windshield and flung into the air, rolling over the roof and onto the ground.

The car didn't even slow down. If anything, it sped up. Seconds later, it was out of sight. "Get help!" I screamed. "NOW!"

Damien's friends ran into the school, yelling incoherently. Charlie and I rushed to try and help Damien. His face was awash with blood. I took my jacket off, lifted his head and laid it back down gently on top of my jacket.

"I'm so sorry," I stuttered. "You're going to be alright." He trembled, shivered. He opened his mouth to speak. "Don't talk," I told him, my voice cracking. "You're going to have plenty of time for that later."

"I need an ambulance now," Charlie was saying into his phone.

His voice slippery, Damien persisted in his endeavour to tell me something. "No, really," I said. "Don't try to speak."

"I'm sorry," he managed, blood spraying out of his mouth. "I'm sorry for everything."

"Don't be," I said, all anger and hatred gone. "You're going to be okay. You're going to be okay."

"Thank you," he continued, his words raspy and pain-filled. "You're lucky to be loved." His shaking greatly intensified as blood flooded into his lungs and out of his lips.

"You're going to be okay," were the last words he heard as his eyes fell shut, never to open again.

Footsteps were approaching. "HE'S DEAD!" I screamed, my voice strangled. "HE'S DEAD!"

***

I screamed and screamed and screamed. Until I couldn't anymore. I don't remember anything else.

I was ordered by the court to undergo anger management, and complete a community payback order. I was given community service – two-hundred-and-forty hours of unpaid work. I know I needed it, especially the anger management. If it hadn't been for my ferocious fury, Damien Sinclair would still be alive.

He's dead because of me. I'll never forgive myself for what happened. I'll never forgive myself for causing the death of Damien Sinclair.

But there were also others, I think, who played their part.

Damien's funeral was open to the public, for anyone who wanted to pay their respects. More people attended than I had expected.

I'll begin with his father who was utterly ridiculous. His son was dead and he spent the entirety of the funeral looking at his watch. It didn't take a genius to guess he viewed this whole thing as a bothersome inconvenience taking him away from his precious job. Disgustingly, my main memory of the service has nothing to do with Damien. It's to do with the neglect Damien had lived through. I didn't even see Mr Sinclair at the wake. I may be wrong, but I'm convinced he rushed back to work. Damien, his son, was dead … and he sped back to work. Most likely for a meeting.

Having considered Damien's father a tough act to follow in terms of indifference, I was more than infuriated at seeing his mother was going around weeping about how *she* had been affected. Not once did she mention his name. Honestly. It was both disturbing and fascinating.

His brother, who looked about ten years older, simply looked bored, yawning continuously throughout the service. He didn't even come into the wake: he stood outside smoking until his mum left.

I finally understood. Damien bullied in the hope of getting attention and love from his parents and brother. He probably lived his life without even half of the attention I received growing up.

Damien Sinclair may have been a bully, targeting all those weaker than him, but he was hurting himself. Not that that excuses his behaviour, but it explains it. I spent years of my life ignorantly hating him. Maybe things would have turned out differently if I had asked him why, if I had helped him. That was all he needed. That's what we all need: someone who'll love us, who'll listen.

His family failed him. His cronies failed him. The school failed him. *I* failed him.

Damien was a *person*. Flawed, but with redeeming qualities. Only one person spoke lovingly about him: his grandmother. Cowardly, I sat a few rows behind her. I couldn't speak to any of his family:

it was my fault he was dead, after all. I didn't have the nerve. How could I bring myself to speak to any of them?

I'm not sure who was speaking to his grandmother. That wasn't important. What *was* important was how heartbroken she was by his demise.

I shouldn't have eavesdropped, I know, but I wanted to hear about what Damien was truly like. Usually, people are different at home than they are at school or work.

"He shone," she began, her voice bubbly, her eyes stuck to the overly large photograph of Damien. "He was my life when my husband passed over. Damien did everything he could to keep me going. He cooked me meals, spent days upon days at my house. He took care of me when I couldn't look after myself."

My heart twisted as I listened. I had taken her grandson from her. Nothing I ever did would ever bring him back to her. I killed her best friend. His blood is on my hands.

She continued, her voice growing ever more unsteady, "If it hadn't been for my Damien, I would have gone to join my husband long ago. I do not know what I'm going to do now. I'm not going to let all of his hard work go to waste: whatever happens, whatever life throws at me, I'm going to stand tall and refuse to die. For him. His memory will keep me going."

Perhaps being a coward, I decided I couldn't listen to any more without breaking: before the funeral, my conscience had chosen to force me to remain as calm as humanly possible. After all, I killed him. I didn't deserve to be upset at his funeral.

Honestly, I'm not even sure I deserved to be at his funeral, to pay my respects. Despite my guilt, I am so glad I went as it taught me a lesson and punished me at the same time.

I'm in a constant battle though. Even with the court's decision that I was not the cause of his death, rather it was the drunkard behind the wheel, I will carry that guilt with me until my time comes. With it, I will bear the unescapable fact that I know if I hadn't been fighting with Damien, if I had remained calm, he would still be alive.

It's ridiculous that I'm even saying that: Damien's time hadn't come. It was brought to him.

Now, however, I know that people are complicated. They are flawed because of what they go through every day. That old saying is true: "Be kinder than necessary for everyone is fighting a battle of which you know nothing."

Damien lived in turmoil. He died too soon. He didn't get the chance to live out his life, to find out what he was capable of, to realise his potential. I took that away from him.

I'm a murderer and I will have to live with that fact until I die.

Although I know I deserve all the pain I am experiencing and more, I refuse to let it overwhelm me: that would be allowing Damien to die in vain.

I'm going to live out my own life doing everything I can to help the bullied stop being bullied and the bullies stop being bullies.

I have learned that, when things go wrong, you can change for the better. You get stronger. I owe it to Damien to help people like him. I owe it to my brother to help people like him.

Unity and understanding will cure this world.

Final Walk

As I wrote the very first draft of Final Walk at Academy, this one is dedicated to my secondary school friends. Specifically, Jasmine, Rachel, Nadia, Jodie, Erin and Eden.

Today is the day. Today has been widely anticipated by the vile people of Bermand and most likely the rest of this condemned country. Today's event will hit national headlines. Of that, I am certain. How do I know? It's simple really: today is the day of my execution.

My name will live on in infamy. Richard Jackson. Notice it's *my* name going down in villainy. Not the adulteress. Not the hypocrite. Such is the scale of the injustice this country dwells under. I will be remembered as a murderer, a psychopath who showed no remorse.

Being honest – because, unlike the adulteress, I do not lie – I show no remorse because I don't feel any. I am proud of what I have done.

My conscience is clear: I have lived by the word of God. All you have to do is read the twenty-second verse of the twenty-second chapter of Deuteronomy.

This is the story of how I lost everything thanks to the adulterers. I will never see my son, Thomas, again because of their lack of restraint. Hatred rages and burns through me. And I welcome their flames.

It doesn't take a genius to realise this story of mine will never be known. Not that it matters. I will tell it nevertheless.

***

Scorched into my memory are the fourth and fifth of June. At work, I was making sure all the paperwork was in order. Sitting in my wonderful office, I had no recollection of the following fact: it was our eighth wedding anniversary.

It is perfectly ridiculous that I was expected to remember our anniversary on top of everything else I had to do. You see, the adulteress only worked one afternoon a week. A three-hours-long afternoon.

I, on the other hand, worked long hours six days a week. What other option did I have? I needed to put food on the table, clothes on the backs of my relatives. I needed to keep a roof over our heads. I had to earn enough for us to live on. After all, nobody else was going to do it.

Anyway, moving on from that injustice, it was our anniversary. Eight years before, I married the adulteress who stole my life. In total, we spent twelve years, seven months and two days together. A relationship built on the back of lies.

Stupidly, I thought everything was *fine*. We so often do. I knew, of course, the adulteress was taking advantage of me. She forced me to work all those hours to facilitate her own laziness. Doing the best I could for my family, I would return home in the evenings – after working all day, might I add – to have the adulteress screeching about how late I was. Thomas was already in bed, the dinner was cold. Odd how she could not notice her own foibles.

So as not to disobey Ephesians and sin in anger, I studiously ignored her and ate my dinner. After thanking her for the food, I then went for a walk.

When I returned home, the hypocrite's car sat in the drive. Not being an unusual occurrence, I thought nothing of it. He would be giving her the church finances to sort out.

Walking up the path to my house, I heard our bed creak. Assuming the adulteress had called it a night, I headed upstairs. The adulteress lacked common sense: she didn't even have the intelligence to shut the door.

My world crashed around me, showering me with glass shrapnel. Blood hammered in my ears like a gavel on a judge's desk. My heartbeat was out of control. I couldn't breathe.

"You gigolo!" I boomed, loud enough to wake the dead.

I stormed through the room, overturning everything in my path. "You are supposed to be a man of God."

Grabbing him by his hair, I pulled him off the bed and started kicking him in the stomach and head.

I cannot remember what I said. However, my voice echoed in the summer air as I thrust every ounce of rage inside me onto him.

I threw the gigolo down the stairs, onto the street. Squealing in pain, he tried to speak. No doubt hoping to explain his sin away. "No." I spat the word out like venom. "You do *not* get to speak. Get out of my sight. "If I ever see you again," I promised, "you will die."

Whimpering, he crawled into his car.

As I lifted my head, it became clear that the adulterer had clutched the attention of the entire street. Every resident of Mason Crescent stared, unrelenting judgement shining in their eyes. Little did I know then that they were judging me. Hypocrisy!

He drove away.

My recollection after he left is a little hazy. I remember the adulteress apologising, yet trying to force the blame onto me. Although the country knows me as a murderer, the man who burned Reverend Polleon to death in his own home, I know who I am. I am a man of morals, living by the word of God the way most lack the courage to. I have done nothing wrong. I recall her cowering in a corner as I left.

I stayed in a hotel that night, alcohol keeping me company.

***

Now we come to the fifth.

Awoken by an ardent fire in my blood, my head splitting, screams poured out of me. Everything had been ruined. A small collection of empty bottles sat on the hotel's bedside table. Eight in total. One for each year of marriage. My anger had matured.

Out of the window, I had a direct view of the church and a slightly obscured view of the Reverend's house. *How could he have done this?*

Teeming with hatred, I knew his betrayal would not go unpunished. In a whirlwind of detestation, I walked to the nearest petrol station, purchased a can and a lighter. Once I'd filled it, I went to the hypocrite's house.

Knowing his schedule, as everybody in the village did, I knew he would be at the church, penning one of his sermons.

Rather like the adulteress, the hypocrite lacked intelligence. He trusted people to the extent that he never locked his door. And, for some unfathomable reason, he told everyone that. I just walked in.

Pouring the liquid over the furniture, the books, the stairs, the counters, I felt nothing but anger. A twinge of doubt came into my head, but it vanished quickly. The Seventh Commandment had been broken and punishment was nigh.

Walking out of the building, I took the lighter. In a whisky haze, I dropped it. The hypocrite's abode was engulfed in fire.

Nothing less than justice, I thought to myself.

Watching the flames tear through the house, satisfaction flowed through me.

A gurgled scream came from inside the building. Another. Another. Another.

Looking up, I saw the hypocrite at the window. Burning, he tried to open the window. Scream after scream after scream erupted from him. I watched him burn.

"Enjoy Hell," I said.

Someone came running up behind me. Ralph Poulter, the hypocrite's secretary. "The firemen are coming, along with the police!" he cried. "Don't worry, I called them. They will find whoever did this."

Then, he heard the screams. "Justice will prevail. He cannot be saved," I replied.

CREAK.

In a great ball of fire, the building collapsed. The hypocrite was dead.

The world was a better place for it. One less hypocrite, one less liar. "Eternal punishment is thine."

Turning to walk away, I heard the blaring sirens. I wasn't trying to get away, I just wanted to sit down. I knew everything would be twisted to make it my fault.

I was right.

So I went to the graveyard next to the church and sat beside my parents' graves. Just sat there. In silence. There was nothing to say. They knew it all. My parents knew the truth. If I didn't know they were proud of the man of God I had become, I maybe would regret exacting justice. Maybe. Justice, no matter how difficult, must be served.

Smiling, I looked around. The grass, the cloudless sky, the sun, the warmth. The fifth was a beautiful day. The best day. It marked my first time doing what needed to be done. I loved the adulteress. More than life itself. But, I knew she was not the wife our Lord demanded she should be. I never challenged her on it. Maybe, just maybe, I played a small part in her sin by not putting her in her place.

However, I am proud of what I have done. Justice was finally served. The hypocrite was dead. The adulteress would, I hoped, be ostracised.

Unfortunately for the people of this country, they distanced themselves further from God by siding with the sin of the adulteress and the hypocrite.

Before long, at least six police officers came marching through the graveyard, handcuffs in hand. "Are you Richard Jackson?" they asked. I confirmed their suspicions. "You are under arrest," one of them mumbled.

Out of pure spite, I asked him to repeat himself, telling him not to mumble this time. The fool did so, telling me to get up and put my hands behind my back. "I only obeyed God's word," I answered. "This country should do it more often."

Tightening the handcuffs to an unnecessary degree, the policeman dragged me through the churchyard into the little lane, reading me my rights.

Before they threw me into their vehicle, I turned to the remains of the hypocrite's house of sin, a smile forming on my face. Justice is served, yet injustice survives.

That police car … the only way I can think to describe it is repugnant. Cigarette smoke hung in the air. Another toxin to endure.

What they made me sit on could not have been any more uncomfortable. It was like a jagged rock.

There were no seatbelts. Not that I could have put one on with those ridiculous unnecessary handcuffs. I am not a dangerous man; I am an obedient man. I hurt those who need to be punished. I am justified in all that I do.

It's always the just who suffer, the innocent. *In this world you will have tribulation*, I remembered. The drive took me to Bermand Police Station where I was met with techniques resembling those of Jehu.

From the police car, I was hauled into an interview room. The fools even tried to intimidate me by encircling me like predators. I would not be intimidated.

"Are you Richard Jackson?" an officer yawned. In the obscene brightness of the light, his boredom was amplified. Sitting with his head resting on one hand, the cretin repeated his question.

"Wow," I replied. "You clearly love your job. That must be why you haven't tied your tie properly, or washed."

By means of response, he flicked his hand. Before I could even think about what that was supposed to mean, the brute grabbed me by my hair and threw my head into the table. Warmth trickled from my nose.

Visibly enjoying himself, Officer Cretin again repeated his question. "This time," he tersely hissed, "be careful how you answer." I nodded. "Is that a yes?" he enquired, the boredom in his voice entertaining me to no end.

"Yes." I practically growled the word, spitting it through gritted teeth. I hold no responsibility for being abrupt: when you deal with hypocrites and liars, there is no need to be civil. They suck the civility out of me.

"Worker at Jackson Law Firm?"

What. An. Idiot. It took all of my restraint not to throw myself over the table, wrap my hands around his puny little neck, squeeze my fingers into his throat and watch the life leave him.

"I *am* the firm," I whispered. "I built it from nothing. It took a lot of sacrifices, a lot of time and effort. But I built a life for myself – a life, may I add, better than the sad existence you have."

Ignoring my outburst, Officer Cretin continued, "Where were you this morning at ten-twenty-one?" As he spoke, he scribbled in his little notebook. His penmanship was an embarrassment.

Feeling my smile returning, I told him, "At the hypocrite's abode. Burning it to the ground." At that point, he looked at me, his disgust apparent and his judgement obvious. Clearly, he didn't know how to respond. "I am perfectly justified. Don't you read scripture?"

Confusion contorted Officer Cretin's pathetic face. Luckily for the fool, I obeyed every part of God's word and refused to give the devil any opportunity.

"He slept with my wife. He got what he deserved. I have done nothing wrong. Are we finished?"

A unanimous intake of breath left me howling with laughter. "So," Officer Cretin managed, through aghast gasps. "You burned the house down with our wonderful Reverend inside." It wasn't really a question, it was more of a statement of the obvious. Some people must need to be told things several thousand times before understanding.

"You make it sound like murder. It was justice. You should understand that, being a policeman. Read scripture. Educate yourself. Our once great nation is falling short of God's standard more with each passing day. We need to become right with our Lord again."

I couldn't – and cannot – understand how ignorant these people were. No matter how I try. "You are going to rot in prison, Jackson. Maybe we should read our Bibles more. Particularly Romans Chapter Three. Take this animal to the cells."

Closing his folder, Officer Cretin rose and left.

As soon as he had shut the door, four policemen grabbed me, hoisted me to my feet and dragged me to a cell.

It was inhumanely small. Not that it bothered me: I know Christ's Sermon on the Mount. I know I would be blessed for this persecution.

Hours upon hours trudged by. Standing in the dark, I tried not to think about how Thomas would be raised. Obviously, the adulteress would make him hate me because of her own infidelity, because I obeyed the word of God. My son would now be brought up to believe I was a monster. But I know I will be rewarded for staying true to my faith, obeying God.

Poor Thomas.

Pacing back and forth around my cell was all I could do to keep myself from descending into madness. Back and forth. Back and forth. Back and forth.

A key clanked into the lock of my cell door. It flew open, light temporarily obscuring my view. A silhouette stood in the door, eclipsing the light, drowning me in shadow. Silently, it stood, watching me. Irritation rose within me. *Do not sin,* I warned myself. *Do not give an opportunity to the devil.*

Motionless, for minutes it watched me. "You know I am a good and righteous man of God," I told the shadow. "You know I am justified. Are you here to turn from your sin? To repent? To let me go?"

Putting its hand behind its back, my adversary lashed out with a baton and thundered towards me. Falling to the ground, I curled into a foetal position. Blow after blow after blow after blow. Constant, never-ending.

Unable to move, unable to think, I just lay there. *How could this have happened? I was a good husband, a perfect husband. I was firm, but fair. Faithful. Honest. Loving. Loyal. Why was this happening?*

As the attack continued, I thought about Job. He lost everything. Despite everything he went through though, he stayed true to God, loyal to God and everything turned out well in the end. *That is what will happen here,* I told myself. I believe it. God is good.

Miraculously, no bones were broken. I would not be surprised if my attacker had been told where to strike to avoid breaking them.. Having been a lawyer in Bermand, I knew how rife police brutality was. Nobody spoke up, so nothing apparently happened.

Days went by in which I could hardly walk for the pain. Could barely breathe without my throat tightening. All I could do was remember Jesus Christ came before me and experienced all the hatred and violence this world had to offer. Yet, He still loves us, forgives us.

In Hs name, I tried to forgive them. I did not retaliate, though I could have.

I didn't sleep well in that cell. My pain was too extreme; slumber stealthily eluded me. As nights dragged on, I would pray for justice to return to the country, the world, for Thomas, even for the adulteress. I prayed that she would raise Thomas properly. I even prayed for the policemen, that they would learn restraint and turn from their sins.

In spite of everything I had lost, no tears came. I would not cry. Crying would show weakness.

***

Being totally honest, I do not know how long I spent there. All the days merged into one. It could have been a week, a month, a year. Either way, eventually, it was time to go to court.

As I confessed in the interview, there would be no trial. Instead, my court appearance would be a sentencing. My lack of interest could not have been hidden, so I didn't try.

For some obscure, illogical reason, they assigned me a lawyer … I *am* a lawyer. A much better one than Stephen Crowe. Although we had never met before, we knew of each other and disliked one another with a passion: our firms were competitors. Of course, mine always came out on top. We were rivals. That was probably why they assigned him to me. Another blow.

Crowe sat down in the chair beside mine with an unsubtle smirk across his idiotic face. He stared while I tossed a pen from hand to hand. Being fair to me, I had to think of something to lessen the boredom I was experiencing. Everything takes so long. Especially when the judge is a known alcoholic. Apparently, he was the only judge willing to take the case. All the other city judges wanted to watch me be sentenced from the public gallery.

After a minute or so of enduring Crowe's unblinking stares, I turned to him. "Is there something I can help you with?"

Something else I cannot fathom: how shocked he looked at my lack of interest. I knew how it would go and I didn't care. I had already lost everything important to me. The best I could hope for was a life sentence.

"At least pretend to be sorry for what you have done," he muttered under his breath. "It might help your case. It might help you get a lighter —"

"Let me stop you right there. I do not lie. I am not sorry for what I did. I was justified. I was obedient. I have lost everything I care about. I hope to be sentenced to death."

Rolling his eyes, Crowe sat in silence.

Bermand's courtroom – a chamber I had seen dozens, if not hundreds of times – had never looked so dissimilar. The glittering chandelier hanging oh, so elegantly from the ceiling, the dark oak floors, the Bermand emblem (an eagle spreading its wings to take flight) sitting mounted on the wall behind the Judgement Seat. And, in front of me stood the ridiculously over-sized desk at which Judge Lewis Desmond now sat.

He could not have looked any less sober if he had tried. His massive body slumped grotesquely. The hatred of my once godly city was falling on me. I could sense it, feel it. I lived in a city of God-fearing hypocrites: ostensibly, the whole pack of them were outstanding Christians. Give them any chance, however, and they would show you the venom running through their veins, the hatred in their blood.

"Richard Jackson," Desmond slurred, "you waived your right to a trial with your written confession." *Written? More lies from Bermand's hypocrites.* "You sentence will not be nearly as severe as I wish I could make it." I couldn't help but laugh.

"Does something strike you as funny, Jackson?"

I nodded. "Several things, Desmond." I had passed the point of caring what happened to me. Something within me had snapped as I realised how absurd this situation was, how unjust. My reputation had been eradicated due to the adulteress's infidelity, but she would walk away unscathed. "My first point is this: you need to be more professional. Turning up to court drunk is not policy, or moral. Second, it is the height of hypocrisy and lunacy that I am in court to receive a criminal sentence when all I did was obey God's word."

Swinging around, I surveyed the crowd, looking for the adulteress.

"Jezebel is in attendance," I announced, pointing at her. "She promised before God to stay with me, and me alone, until death parts us. Eight years later, I found her with the so-called man of God who officiated at our wedding."

With every word I spat, the fury within me intensified. Audible gasps flew around the courtroom as I turned back to face the drunk. "If I had the chance to kill him over again, I would do so with pride. Polleon deserved it. And he knew it. Can I borrow your Bible?"

After looking around, as if for permission, Desmond reluctantly handed it to me. Glaring at the adulteress, I flicked to the book of Leviticus. "The man that committeth adultery with another man's wife, the adulterer and the adulteress shall be put to death," I read.

Handing the Bible back, it was impossible not to feel hundreds of eyes sinking into my skin like blades. "There's one left."

I launched across the barrier, sprinting with outstretched arms, towards the Jezebel. At the very most, I moved ten steps before dozens of officers tackled me to the ground. "I will kill you. You hear? I will kill you!"

"Get him out!" Desmond shouted.

While they pulled me away, my eyes stayed on Jezebel. *I will kill her. I will kill her.*

They left me in a padded room and handcuffed me to a table. I prayed for justice to prevail.

When the officers returned, they looked uneasy, as though they thought I might attack them. *Idiots.*

I knew what was coming next and I was ready for it. Leading me back to court, an officer snarled, "You are going down.. Your name is well-known and no-one inside will let you live a day.

"Are you sure they have spelt it correctly?"

Flanked by three weedy little men, I stood before the judge one final time. Crowe had been useless. His professional opinion was that I deserved all I got.

Plonking himself down in his seat, with a tone shrouded in melodrama, Desmond declared: "Richard Jackson, you have portrayed an outdated, and frankly perverse, understanding of justice. Displaying no remorse for your brutality, you have shown no respect for this court. I sentence you to life in prison. Take him away."

Another miscarriage of justice: everyone has a right to appeal. May as well get this life over with though. I didn't protest. I welcomed the sentence.

***

So that's my story. I maintain that I've done nothing wrong because I know the truth. My life lies in ruins. I long for the lightning. I anticipate it. I am not apologetic for the righteous act I performed. I obeyed the word of God.

We will all be judged according to our actions and I cannot wait.

I have made the preparations. I will not be here for much longer. The bed sheet is ready – the knot tied. May God have mercy on your souls.

Mad as a Hatter

Dedicated to the sensational Margot Wood. Thank you for everything.

Quill scratching parchment could be heard from outside.

Abel had not been seen in public for several days, not even on the week's third day, which was strange considering his relentless determination to tell the children of Wonderland about the tales his closest friend – well, only friend – Jehoia, had written. Every week, for three years, without fail, Abel had read to the children. Because of this, everybody knew something was wrong. But, he wouldn't tell anybody, no matter how much they asked – not even Jehoia knew what was wrong. He wouldn't tell anyone. He would not endanger them.

Have to finish. Have to finish. Have to finish.

He had received a summons from Queen's Palace for the evening meal. Nobody in their right mind declined a summons. That would mean death.

Abel would not have been so determined to finish if he had not known something was going to happen to him. He just knew. Usually, on the very rare occasion, when somebody was summoned by the infamously bloodthirsty Queen of Hearts, they had to make their own way to her lair.

He, however, would be escorted by her most esteemed soldiers. Why? He didn't know.

He didn't fear death though. What worried him was the thought of never being able to disclose the truth to Wonderland, the truth about its monarchy.

He came to the end of his document and quickly scribbled his name. Without even putting the quill back, Abel galloped out of his home and across the street to thump manically on Jehoia's door.

She ran to answer his incessant knocking.

"Why must you bang like that? Are you having a seizure?"

Although they had been best friends their entire lives, Abel had a tendency to infuriate Jehoia. He loved her, simply adored everything about her. He loved the way her flowing ginger hair blew back in the soft wind. He lived for the way her green eyes reminded him of the fields in the valleys of Academy where they'd met.

Located in the small dip between two colossal mountains, the Academy was for only the smartest of Wonderland.

Exotic and honourable though it might be, if deemed eligible to become a student there, you would be taken from your family at birth and never know them.

The Elders of Wonderland were made aware of one's eligibility through the Purple Storm. Rain hammers down only around the home of a particular newborn child and the lightning is brightest there. Once the storm is at its most violent, the Elders ride into the eye and return to Academy with the baby. This occurrence is seldom: only two eligible children are born in a decade.

Abel's crazed expression didn't change as he handed her the manuscript.

"What's this?" she asked, riddled with concern, making to turn some pages.

Abel slammed his hand down on the parchment so roughly he almost hit it out her hand. "Don't look at it unless I do not return tonight."

Regret swept over him like scolding water then for being so harsh.

Jehoia, despite her dominating personality, knew better than to question Abel though when he was in this state.

"Do you want to come in for a drink?" she enquired, clearly feeling unsure of what else to say. He shook his head.

In the near distance, a horse whinnied. Cold sweat dampening his face, Abel swung round, his breathing erratic.

"Why are you so panicked?"

He trembled uncontrollably. Sweat poured off him, forming small puddles at his feet.

"I've been summoned," he rasped.

Jehoia looked at him, obviously trying to think of something consoling to say.

Failing that, she placed the manuscript on the shelf above her fireplace, walked over to Abel and hugged him.

"How are you getting there?" she asked, now shaking too.

"Soldiers," he replied, his voice solemn, crushed. "Could I have a glass of water, please?"

Never before had Abel felt so perfectly destroyed.

Growing up, Abel had had no sense of danger. Jehoia half-smiled.

"What?" Abel said.

"I'm remembering the time you tried to abseil down the Academy wall." It wasn't particularly high. However, Abel was six years old at the time. But now, his spirit laid shattered.

She rushed to get him his drink. When she returned, he drained it with one gulp.

"Thank you," he gasped, handing the glass back.

Clip-clop. Clip-clop. Clip-clop. Clip-clop.

I'm going to die.

The more he thought about it, the more Abel was convinced that Death's Angel was watching over him, planning the perfect way to kill, waiting for the right moment. Oh, how that demon must be enjoying watching him suffer.

Clip-clop. Clip-clop. Clip-clop. Clip-clop. They were getting closer. Closer. Closer. *When would this end? How would this end*?

He turned to Jehoia, wrapping his hand in hers.

"Whatever happens," he whispered, "remember I love you. I always have and I always will."

Weakly smiling, Jehoia answered, "I love you too." How she managed to remain composed, to keep her voice from betraying heartache, he did not know. "Don't worry," she continued. "We will see each other again."

Abel wasn't certain if she was speaking to him or herself.

Trumpets echoed in the dim light of early evening. Within moments they would arrive. Jehoia tightened the handhold, as did Abel.

He blinked and, when he opened his eyes, they were there. There in front of them, clothed in white, with a ruby-red heart in the centre of their attire, sitting high upon horses, black as burnt paper. Six soldiers of Wonderland.

"You," one of them said, his voice cruel, unforgiving. "The Queen of Hearts is waiting." Turning his horse away and beginning to walk off, he finished with: "And she's not patient at the best of times."

Jehoia, still holding onto Abel's hand almost as tenaciously as he was holding onto hers, stepped forward, betraying no fear.

"What is this about?" she asked.

The soldier who had spoken dismounted, pulled out his sword and held it less than an inch away from her face.

"I do not answer the questions of peasants. You will do well to learn some respect."

Jehoia's heart pounded viciously in her chest, as though it were trying to burst out.

"You have such a pretty house," he continued, his voice now mocking, condescending. "I would hate for something to happen to it.

He turned to Abel. "Hurry up, street urchin." Her Majesty's vile soldier returned to his horse, without taking his eyes off Jehoia.

She kissed Abel on the cheek, let go of his hand and watched, tears filling her eyes, as he walked further and further away until she could no longer see the one she loved.

Sobbing, she walked back into her home and closed the door. When the door was shut, she fell to the ground in a burst of hysterical tears.

***

Abel walked all three miles to the palace on uneven ground, flanked by two horsemen, beside two others and behind two more. No chance of escape. Besides, even if he tried, he wouldn't be able to outrun the horses. Plus, what trouble would it bring to Jehoia? What troubles would it bring the rest of

Wonderland? Jehoia had already been threatened, just for speaking up for him.

The night was unbearably humid. It hadn't rained for days and the temperature had been steadily rising since the beginning of the previous week. He wished now he hadn't drank his water so quickly: his throat was already starting to dry.

Silence prevailed for the duration of their journey to the palace, adding significant tension to Abel's already disquieted mind. He tried desperately to think of something other than the ways in which the Queen of Hearts could rip his life away from him. How she could torture him.

She could hang him from the towers with ropes dipped in chemicals. She could sever his limbs one by one. Wonderland's monarch could do whatever she wanted. Nothing could stop her, nobody.

Trying to console his raging heart, he reminded himself he was only twenty-one. *Why does that matter when she has killed younger folk?*

A question entered his mind: why was she wanting to see him? There was only one rational answer he could formulate: she knew he was aware of the truth. He knew she wasn't who she said she was. *But how did she know? How could she know?*

Abel kept his suspicion as close to him as he could. Nobody knew. Unless Jehoia had read the document which, he assumed, she probably had.

No, he thought to himself, *she can't possibly know.*

Can she?

Questions piled on him until he felt like he was being buried alive. Abel was suffocating under their magnitude. *Was somebody spying on him? If so, why?* And, the most important question: *Am I being paranoid?*

He hoped, against all odds, that delusion had set in and he was being irrational. Despite his attempts to grasp these hopes, he knew he wasn't though.

She *knew.*

They marched ever closer to the palace. He knew because of the silence of his surroundings. Even at night, birds sang in Wonderland. But there are places even birds won't go. As he scanned his surroundings, he saw no animals, no people and heard no sound.

Yes, he was nearing death.

Wonderland Palace sat atop a hill, giving the monarchs the ability to survey their domain. This, Abel thought, was just another way to instill fear into the citizens.

As the journey slugged on, the ground became steeper. The incline was unforgiving, growing more perilous with every step. The silence felt unnatural, unsettling. Nothing could have prepared him for this and nothing could prepared him for what lay ahead.

Abel's vision blurred thanks to dehydration and exhaustion. He began to stumble.

"Water," he gasped. "Please."

Most of the soldiers continued on as if he hadn't spoken. One, however, gave him a sip of water from the flask hanging from his saddle.

"Thank you," Abel mouthed, hoping the soldier could see his face in the dim moonlight.

Walking and breathing with any steadiness grew more difficult the higher they climbed. The castle loomed above him, casting long shadows.

Although they were not in complete darkness, Abel's internal and external unease could not be quelled. Intense black walls cloaked the courtyard.

Probably cemented with the blood of murdered innocents, Abel thought.

As they neared, there were glowing red circles shining through the gates.

The Queen's Pack, Abel realised, his legs threatening to buckle. *I'm never getting out of here.*

Her Majesty's Pack consisted of eight wolves of the Nuit Forest. All of Wonderland knew these animals and everyone feared them. Growling, with drool dripping from their lips, the wolves parted, forming a walkway as the gates creaked open.

The group of soldiers marched forward, themselves now visibly trembling too. Only the leader remained calm, walking on with a toothy grin.

Abel couldn't have moved any quicker without running.

The courtyard was lit by flaming lanterns which spewed sparks across its inner square. Terror grabbed Abel by the neck, digging in its curled nails. He couldn't think of anything other than how petrified he was, how doomed he was, how much he wanted to see Jehoia again.

They walked by a staircase which Abel assumed lead to the dungeon. Abel heard the tortured screams of its prisoners, felt their anguish, recognised the noise of rattling chains. Their cries eroded his mind, burning away all happy memories.

He would more than likely end up in their situation before long. He was as helpless as they were. Not even a flicker of light shone at the bottom of those stairs.

The night's pitch blackness obscured most of Abel's surroundings, adding enormous weight to his fear..

He was marched into the palace and the door shut with a loud bang behind him.

"Blindfold him," a soldier snarled.

In obedience, several people tackled Abel to the ground, tied his hands together and covered his eyes. Feebly, he attempted to fight off his oppressors. His endeavour was carried out in vain though as the more he fought, the severer the opposition became. Fighting was futile. Deep down, he knew that.

The soldiers dragged him up several flights of stairs and along countless corridors. No matter how far through the endless, labyrinthine palace they pulled him, he could not block out the tormented cries of the castle's prisoners which echoed all around.

Eventually, the soldiers removed the blindfold, untied him and threw him into a room. Abel rubbed at his wrists and his eyes. Scanning the room, hoping to find a weapon he could use to defend himself if he needed to, he found nothing.

Of course not, he thought, furious with himself for his stupidity. *They wouldn't leave anything I could use to harm the Queen.*

But where *was the Queen?*

The room consisted of dark red wallpaper and was lit by candelabras lighting, and paintings of the different monarchs of Wonderland had been thrown into the corner.

I was right all along, Abel thought. *If she's taken those paintings down,* he pondered, *she knows.* Defenceless, Abel slumped to the floor. Alone. Completely. Even hope had abandoned him.

Was she deliberately keeping him waiting in an attempt to scare him into submission? Of course. What would she say? Would he ever see Jehoia again?

Jehoia.

Her name brought joy to his mind and pain to his heart. He needed her with him, but he rejoiced in the truth she was safe.

Safety though. Did it exist?

Fear placed a hand on his shoulder. Alone, all he heard was his breathing.

The screams had fallen silent. Were they dead? Or were they resigned to the idea of being alone and therefore had given up trying to be heard?

His senses were in a frenzy. *Get a hold of yourself*, Abel warned himself, although he knew it was no good: he had already passed the point of mental clarity. *Why was this happening?*

Fear plunged its icy blade into him, turning his blood cold.

Where was she?

Abel felt thousands of eyes on him. He was being watched. Somehow. He would *not* break. *Bit late for that though,* he chastised himself. No, he would *not* break.

Silence.

Silence.

Silence.

This eerily dark chamber filled Abel with a strange sense of hope somehow though: the infamously bloodthirsty Queen of Hearts would not kill him quietly in a remote corner of the palace. If she was planning on ending his life, it would be a public spectacle to show Wonderland who to fear. *So*, he thought, *why am I here*?

He immediately regretted asking himself that question though as it brought on another: if she's not going to kill him, what *would* she do?

Before he could think any further, someone thundered towards him down a nearby corridor.

The door flung open, crashing into the wall. "Make way for Her Majesty, The Queen of Hearts."

***

For such an infamous and feared murderer, the Queen of Hearts was miniscule. Moments passed in which Abel could focus on nothing other than her height. He found it laughable, but didn't dare betray his amusement.

Her hair, bright as flaming coals, was tied in a tight bun. Her crown, ostentatious as she was, sent a message to everyone in attendance. She wore an *absurdly* oversized sapphire-blue gown.

"Leave us," she commanded. Her voice was cold. Unloving. Apathetic. Proud.

Staring intently at Abel as she spoke, her eyes searched him. All soldiers departed and shut the door as quietly as they could – most likely so as not to anger the beast before him.

"I assume you know why you're here," she said, clearly trying to fight back a giggle. Something about her eyes unsettled Abel, though he didn't know what. He did his best to avoid them.

"This ridiculous hat," she snarled, chucking the crown onto the table.

Abel opened his mouth, although no words came out. Just a pathetic wheeze escaped.

"You claim to be a genius, yet you can't work out why I've brought you here. That's disappointing."

Finally finding his voice, Abel snapped, "Well, why *am* I here, Your Majesty?"

In response, the Queen snickered. "I can hear venom pouring out of you. You know why you're here. You've been writing about it."

He bombarded himself with questions. *How could she possibly know what I'm writing about? Who does she have watching me? Are any of us safe?*

Does any moment pass when we're not being watched?

Despite all his questions, he could only say, "I see."

"You are, of course, correct," his adversary continued. "I am not the true Queen of Hearts. My name is Adeola Haman. I am *the* assassin of Wonderland. I killed the Princess." There was a sickening pride in her tone, becoming more evident with every word. "Life can be taken with the flick of a hand and hers was." Her lips curved into a narcissistic grin, spreading from ear to ear.

"How did you get away with it?" Abel enquired, his eyes darting from wall to wall as he searched for a way to escape.

Adeola looked at him, her eyes disappointed. "You *are* joking, aren't you?" Abel shook his head, raised his eyebrows. "Genius must be overrated," the assassin replied condescendingly. "Wonderland's law states that, '*No person may see the heir to the throne until the day of coronation.*' It is truly embarrassing that you don't know this."

As she spoke, Adeola paced, asserting her dominance by marking out her territory.

"So, you killed her," Abel said, scanning the room desperately for another exit. "Why?"

"For the throne obviously," she said, laughing. "For power."

Abel shook his head again, completely disgruntled by Adeola's ignorance.

"There are other ways to get power, you know," he snapped. For a split second, he felt bravery flowing through his blood. And, like blood, it spilled out of him.

"BRING MY FOOD!" Adeola bellowed, her voice shrill and piercing.

At least two dozen people suddenly marched into the chamber, each one carrying a dish. Within seconds, the table was set with mountainous platters of food, at least four candlesticks and eight opulent goblets covered in jewels.

Abel's eyes watered with overwhelm at the injustice of it all: people across Wonderland starved and yet this imposter monarch bathed in wealth.

Wonderland's assassin had devoured her first plateful before Abel had even started his own. Adeola gulped down her drink, sounding like a bath emptying.

"Eat, peasant," she hissed.

"I may be a peasant," Abel snarled, "but I have more class than you."

His food tasted odd. That is the only way to describe it. Odd. His first bite left him disorientated. His second dried his throat like a drought dries land. He grabbed his goblet and took a gargantuan gulp. He swallowed and descended into a strained fit of coughing.

"What have you done?" he cried, his throat stinging. Unable to control himself, he thrashed in pain.

"I've poisoned you. Isn't that obvious?" she said, giggling. You were so busy panicking that you didn't pay attention. I can't have you telling anybody who I am. Yes, I'm the most infamous assassin in Wonderland's history." Her pride returned. "If you had been born in the slums of this pathetic place, you would have done anything to get out. Just like I did. I didn't want that life. You don't choose the life you're given, but you get to choose how you live it. I chose to get out and I did."

She stood up so violently her chair fell. Uncaring, she marched around the room.

"I never knew my parents. They sold me to Laosta. Have you heard of him?" All pride had now vanished from Adeola's voice. In its place was a mixture of hurt, grief, anger. Anger mixed with grief is a dangerous thing. It kills.

Abel shook his head. "Who is he?" he enquired, despite not particularly caring. "I never knew my parents. And I never will," he continued "I didn't turn into an assassin though, thriving on the suffering of others."

"You mean, who *was* he?" Adeola said, ignoring Abel's finishing remark. "He was the master of killers. Skills unmatched. Until he taught me everything he knew. I was a natural. He sent us all out on assignments, saving his most important for me." Pausing, she walked to the other side of the table, picked up a knife and twirled it with her fingers. "My aim was, and is, impeccable."

Adeola scanned the room. "The head of the painting over there," she stated simply, pointing to the portrait of the late princess and hurling the knife out of her hand. It found its mark, splitting through all the paintings exactly where she said it would. "As you can see."

Abel swirled round in his chair, stunned by her sudden change in attitude.

"Yes," he began, unsure of where he was going. "I can." His throat screamed as he spoke. "I'm impressed," he continued. "Now, where is the antidote?"

Adeola smiled a twisted, cruel, unforgiving smile. "Oh, don't think that, just because I'm opening up to you, I'm going to let you have the antidote. Once it has bitten, a snake offers no healing."

The rate of Abel's breathing intensified. Death was calling his name. Regrets flooded into his mind. He would *never* know his parents. He had always acknowledged this fact, but never truly understood it. He would never know where he came from. Jehoia. He was never going to see her again. His life was a string of regrets. A tear rolled down his cheek. *At least,* he thought, *it will be quick.*

"Do not think, however," the Queen continued, "that I'm going to show you the courtesy of allowing you to die. The poison you just drank will take thirty minutes to complete its work."

Hope waned, Abel replied, "What will it do to me?" His voice now weak and he sounded helpless.

"You're the genius," she answered, smirking. "You tell me."

Abel stared down, screwing his face up as he tried to think. And tried to think. And tried to think. "I don't know," he said, utterly defeated.

"Keep trying to think," Adeola goaded, putting emphasis on the word "trying".

It hit him. "You've stolen my mind," he cried, his words catching in his throat. "I'm going to lose my mind."

"You'll be as mad as a hatter in less than an hour," Adeola said, giggling. "Anyway," she continued. "Laosta assigned me the task of killing the Princess of Hearts. Her father had died and she would take the throne two weeks later. Laosta was going to take the throne. Nobody knew the sex of the royal baby. I used this to my advantage." Again, she paused to melodramatically look around. "But, as I have said, I didn't exactly choose this life. I did what I had to do to remove myself from the slums."

She looked at Abel expectantly. "What was that?" he asked, smiling manically and trying desperately not to laugh. *Why am I so happy? Does it matter? The point is, I am.* "Hello!"

194

He spoke slowly, dragging the word out. "What did you do?"

Adeola continued, "I slaughtered them, spending the most time on Laosta. He was the only person to fight back. After I had butchered the people I had grown up with, I fled the scene, running to this palace."

"That's funny," Abel said, snickered, suddenly, for some reason, genuinely amused. "Hey!" he yelled. "I'm rich." He proceeded to pick up a golden goblet and tried to hide it in a pocket he did not have.

"That night, the skies opened and the rain came down in torrents. I slid through the town unseen. Nobody notices what they don't want to see. Knife in hand, I strolled up to the palace, ready to attack," Adeola said. "No guards stood at the gates; I could have walked straight through. However, I could hear talking from the other side of the wall. Wanting a challenge, I scaled the walls, slitting the throats of the guards on landing."

Abel jumped off his chair, laughing hysterically. "When is your birthday?" he managed, between bursts of uncontrollable giggles.

Ignoring him, Adeola spoke again. "Ridiculous. A fifteen-year-old taking out the Royal Guards." She walked round the room as she spoke, her smile ever widening as she ventured further into her story. "After they were dead, I marched through the palace, butchering everyone in sight. I suppose I should feel remorse, but I don't. Weaklings are a waste. Not one of them tried to fight back."

Abel danced cheerfully around the room, singing Wonderland's anthem, unaware Adeola was still speaking. All fear had vanished, as had his mind.

Unperturbed, the Queen of Hearts carried on, "The Princess, to be fair, was beautiful. Her auburn hair, her chocolate-brown eyes, though terrified, were still gorgeous. I'm not evil, believe me. I wanted to spare her, but one has to do what one can to get what one wants. And she had the thing I wanted. I think she knew her time had come. As the lightning came, I raised my sword over her head and brought it crashing down. I spent the rest of the night disposing of the bodies."

Adeola walked over to the window and flung it open.

A waft of heat hit Abel, not that he really could feel it: he was too involved in his dancing. "As you can see, my palace is huge in every way. I only had to kill one eighth of the people and nobody noticed. Brilliant luck, really. You know – sorry, knew – the rest. I'm finished now. Get out. GUARDS!"

As the guards piled into the room, ready to obey Adeola's every demand and Abel's flamboyant gestures ceased.

"What can we do for you, Your Majesty?" a guard managed, his voice quaking along with his body.

"Take this Mad Hatter," she ordered, pointing apathetically at Abel, "and make sure he gets back to his village. He has had a little too much to drink."

"Yes, Your Majesty."

Every guard rushed to follow the Queen's orders, seizing Abel by the scruff of his neck and dragging him out of the room.

When alone, Adeola laughed triumphantly.

***

The guards tossed Abel into a carriage and rode him back to his village. There to meet him stood

Jehoia. She took him inside, closing her door without saying a word to the Queen's staff.

Her home was dim, lit only the moon. It *was* the middle of the night, after all. Abel looked into his friend's eyes intently, but did not recognise her. "What is your name?" he asked. "I am... why, I don't know who I am, but I'm happy."

Jehoia's blood ran cold and her eyes watered. The hurt only those who have been in love can know.

"What has she done to you?" she asked, petrified.

"What has who done to who, dear?" Abel replied, smiling broadly. "You're very pretty." He stood up. "Let's make fire!" he sang.

Tears streaming down her cheek, her heart breaking more and more, Jehoia walked over to Abel, knowing she had lost him forever.

"Sit down, Abel," she said, gently leading him to his favourite armchair next to the candle. "I'll light it for you." She cried silently as she did so.

Jehoia sat next to him, holding his hand, shaking as the love of her life fell asleep. "I love you," she whispered.

Abel awoke several hours later. Seeing the fire beginning to die, he marched over to it. Resting above it was a pile of papers. He tossed them into the flames and, laughing, watched as the truth disappeared, never to be known.

ACKNOWLEDGEMENTS

The first people I need to acknowledge are the family members who always believed in me, always kept me going, kept me writing even when I wanted to give up. Thank you so much.

I would not be where I am now if I hadn't had teachers who believed in me, and helped me improve my writing. Thank you to Mrs Mathers, Mrs Hall, Mrs Robertson, Mrs Mani, Mr Wilson, Mrs Birnie, Miss Shewan, Mr Jones, Mrs Esslemont, Miss Barkham and Miss Bruce.

Special thanks to Miss Gavigan, for showing me the power of words, and for encouraging me to write. Even when I didn't want to.

I would also like to thank Marek, Eilidh, Agne, Dave, Andrea, Mark, Rachel, Josef, Andy, Edgaras, Jay and Jude for all the support you have given me over the years.

I don't know where I would be if it hadn't been for Tomi Adeyemi. Tomi – thank you for being a light in the darkness, for inspiring me to get Miscellany finished, and for motivating me to fight my demons. Thank you for giving me the strength to fight them, thank you for all the hugs. Thank you for your support and thank you for who you are.

Sasha Alsberg, thank you for everything. Thank you for being such a beacon. Thank you for helping me through my Depression with your YouTube. You are an inspiration. Thank you also for the hugs.

Thanks are also due to Lindsay Cummings who taught me that dreams come true, for being a fantastic role model to me and so many others. You are going to be an amazing mother!

Thank you to V.E. Schwab for being you, and for telling me you cannot edit a blank page. To this day, your advice is the best I've ever received.

Sara Holland, thank you for your words, which reminded me why I wanted to write, and why I love to read.

Thank you to all the authors who inspired me to follow my dreams, who got me into reading with their writing: Sarah J Maas, Susan Dennard, Leigh Bardugo, Marie

Lu, Victoria Aveyard, Amy Tintera, Danielle Paige, Natalie Banks, Kristen Martin, Kim Chance and Jenna Moreci.

Special thanks to my greatest friends, without whom, I would cease to exist: Josh, Jaden, Dev, Trendon, Ava, Abigail, Susanna, Matthew, Sam and Malakai.

Thank you to Martin, Scott and the Hillview Young Adults, for always being there, and for making me a better person.

Sharon Zink, thank you so much for your relentless enthusiasm when editing Miscellany.

Last, but certainly not least, thank you so much to you, reader. Thank you for picking up Miscellany.

44062030R00116

Printed in Poland
by Amazon Fulfillment
Poland Sp. z o.o., Wrocław